WE
ALL
FALL
DOWN

**THE FIRST CRACK
IN THE SIMULATION**

WE ALL FALL DOWN

THE FIRST CRACK IN THE SIMULATION

ZOEY SWEET

We All Fall Down

Copyright © 2026 by Zoey Sweet

All rights reserved.

No part of this publication may be reproduced, distributed, or transmitted in any form or by any means, including photocopying, recording, or other electronic or mechanical methods, without the prior written communication of the author, except as permitted by U.S. copyright law. For permission requests, contact hello@zoeysweet.com.

This is a work of fiction. Names, characters, places, and incidents either are the product of the author's imagination or are used fictitiously. Any resemblance to actual people, living or dead, events, or locales is entirely coincidental.

First published April 2026

ISBN 978-1-971103-01-3 (paperback)
ISBN 978-1-971103-00-6 (ebook)

Cover and interior design by Katy Lei

*To my mom
for encouraging
this book to
even happen
in the first place*

CONTENT WARNINGS

War
Terrorism
Bombs
Fires
Death
Torture
Blood
Medical experimentation
Needles
Captivity
Drugging
Alcoholism
Underage drinking
Suicidal ideation
Hallucinations
Broken family
Cheating
Slut-shaming
Sexuality mentions
Menstruation
Bullying
Reckless driving
Driving without a license
Swearing

PROLOGUE

There was once a family of two kids and two parents, and they were happy.

There was also a grandma and grandpa who cared about their grandchildren so very much.

The parents wanted to revisit their old honeymoon days, and what better way than to ask the grandparents to help care for the kids?

The grandparents were excited, driving up with bundles of suitcases and packages. The kids sat by the window, hands moving with glee when the car pulled up. The children loved them all being together, three generations under one roof.

But then it was time. The mom and dad began packing up, stuffing things into bags. The grandparents moved in, placing the grandpa's medical wires and tubes on the nightstand where the family photo of four always rested. They moved the photo into the drawer below. We'll put it back when we leave, the grandparents said. It's only a photo.

The robe that the mom always hung on the coat hook was thrown into a bag and replaced with the grandma's purple and orange pajamas. But those are tiny things, the older kid said in hushed whispers when the lights were long out. They won't replace Mom and Dad.

But the younger one wasn't so convinced. Maybe they were going to love the honeymoon so much that they'd never want to leave. Maybe they'd crash the car on the way to their honeymoon and die forever.

Dreams of their parents floating up into the clouds haunted both the kids at night. Their screams, in turn, tormented the parents in their sleep, wondering what could be so wrong.

The day of departure arrived, and the four hands wouldn't let go. It's only a weekend, and we'll call twice a day, the parents promised. The older one was reassured, but the younger one was far from being quelled. We'll see you very soon, the parents tried. The younger one stopped screaming and looked them both in the eyes, her words scaring everyone in earshot.

No, you won't. Goodbye forever.

But they left anyway. Some may say the younger one was a bit dramatic. They were only eight years of age anyway, but it still shook the family of four as they went their separate ways.

For only a weekend. Or maybe more.

The first hours were tense. The younger one refused to speak to any of them, feeling betrayed by the older one and the grandparents. It dragged on. No words came out of their mouths during lunch. Only obnoxiously loud chewing and the ear-splitting scraping of forks were heard. The fill-in parents said nothing of it, acting as if the kids weren't there.

Nightfall came. Stars filled up the pool of navy blue. *Have they called* was asked over and over again. But the same two-lettered answer prevailed, taking different forms each time it was spoken. They haven't called yet. Then came the classic, maybe they forgot. I can try to remind them. When the digital clock struck eight thirty, nobody had called. We'll try again in the morning, so try to get a good night's sleep.

In the younger one's dreams, flashes of fog took them away, which made two pairs of eyes unable to sleep afterwards. I'll miss you, the younger one said to the darkness. I'll miss you when it all goes away.

The older one listened but said nothing, unsure of what was meant, yet knowing something was going to happen. They both knew that everything would change. Not in the way that a new toy changes what you play with, but in the way that a scar changes the way your face looks.

And they were right.

"I PROMISE! CALM DOWN, OR I SWEAR I'll drown you in that puddle," Ariella said to Daisy as they walked to school. The puddle looked up at them, showing two girls: one with a foot nearing its muddy edge and the other repulsed.

"You can't drown someone in a puddle," Daisy shot back, swinging her emerald braids from side to side.

Ariella thought about it for a second, but she decided to stomp her foot in the water. Hard.

The water sloshed up, and Daisy immediately went over to the side to avoid it. "Ariella!" Daisy whined. "You act just like a little kid sometimes."

Ariella looked at the water on her pant legs before saying, "I'm a three-year-old at heart! Too young and innocent for this world."

Daisy brushed the drops of water off her sweats as she snorted, "Innocent is not a word I'd pick to describe you." Her friend ignored that last bit, jumping onto the road to splash into yet another puddle. Daisy made sure to give her plenty of space as she continued her puddle hunting. "Ariella, we're sophomores this year, not preschoolers."

Ariella gave her a pointed look. "It's the first rain of the season. Everything's nice and fresh and full of life. It would be a waste not to play in the puddles."

"By full of life, you mean cloudy and dismal and ugly, sure," Daisy muttered under her breath, looking at the ground as she made an effort to step over all the cracks.

Ariella sauntered over to her and put a hand on her shoulder, soaked and everything. "Everything okay, Dais?"

Daisy removed Ariella's wet arm. "I'm just kind of stressed. You do remember we have a test in Ms. Shwartz's class, right?"

Ariella stopped and gave her a once-over. "No, today is review day. We watched a movie last class."

"We're being tested on what the movie was about. That was our review," Daisy stated flatly. "I'm pretty sure we're both gonna flunk it."

Ariella stopped in her tracks, eyes wide with horror. "You're kidding. I barely even took notes!"

Daisy shook her head. "That's because you're a grade freak. I'm sure no one in the class took notes."

"I think I'll go and crawl in a hole," Ariella moaned, ignoring Daisy's previous comment. "Just cover me up with dirt before the test and wake me up after."

Daisy tossed her braids over one shoulder before saying in a tone she reserved for freakouts just like this, "If I'm about to drop my GPA, I don't wanna do it alone."

Ariella slumped against someone's mailbox, refusing to take another step. "My parents will murder me." She stopped, thinking through her next words. "Let's go into our holes now so they'll have no one to suffocate."

"Suffocate? I don't think your parents would be so generous." Daisy used one of her hands to grab Ariella by the arm and the other to rub her own chin. "They'd stab you, burn the body, then use a high-powered laser beam to disintegrate the ashes."

"They aren't that bad," Ariella told her, glaring holes into the back of her head. "They just really care about my future." Daisy made sure to look up at the gray and cloudy sky to avoid the look Ariella was giving her. "I like the rain," Ariella said suddenly, changing the subject away from school. "It's like the earth is cleaning itself of all the dirt."

"But there's still dirt on the ground," Daisy reminded her flatly. "Or there wouldn't be earth and mud for you to step in."

Ariella crossed her arms, deep in thought. "The rain wets the dirt to help grow plants and rejuvenate everything around us," she said slowly, "so I guess we're both right."

They both walked in a comfortable silence for a little while, Ariella thinking about the rain and Daisy about the previous night. Their school and its sandstone pillars loomed ominously in the distance. Out front, there was a large sign made of gold and marble telling you that, yes indeed, you'd arrived at *Cliffdale High School*. The walkway to the main entrance was pure white cement, although it was covered at the moment by rain and kids trying to get inside the school. The grass on either side of the walkway was always green, the raindrops making it sparkle like emeralds. It was at this entrance that you could see the perfectness of all three floors: high, higher, and highest. It looked like a fairytale.

It was extremely annoying to Ariella that everyone told their parents to drop them off at that particular entrance. They had four different places to drive up to and more than a dozen entrances, but of course, none were as grand as this one.

"Why do we do this?" Daisy muttered. Ariella was pretty sure that she was referring to both her own previous statement and the horde of kids gathered around. "Why don't we just, I don't know, live like cavemen?"

"But we don't know how to cook," Ariella countered. "We'd be stuck eating burnt mammoth meat."

"I don't want to eat a mammoth," Daisy agreed. She ran her hands through her hair, removing a braid from where it was stuck around her backpack straps. "What if we lived before the Bomb?"

Ariella gave her a strange look. "How far before? Like ten, twenty years?"

Daisy shook her head, waving her hand behind her. "Like when we were allowed to go outside of the RCS."

"We're not allowed to anyway. It's for our own safety."

"But imagine if we lived in that era!"

"Didn't we just watch a movie about that? Like where everyone was at war all the time?" Ariella asked sarcastically.

Daisy trekked across the grass to the entrance on the side. Nobody really cared about that one anyway, so it was easy to get there without drawing attention to the fact that you weren't supposed to be on the grass. Ariella wasn't even sure why the door was there, but it helped them save time. "But then we wouldn't have school! We'd be able to do things!" Daisy animatedly said.

Ariella gave her friend a concerned look. "People weren't able to leave their houses if they even had one. They were stuck hiding every hour of the day." Her face twisted into a half smile. "You didn't take notes on the movie, did you?"

"As I stated previously, why would a reasonable person take notes on a movie?" Daisy opened the school door before continuing, "You'd better let me look at your notes."

"I only have a page and a half," Ariella told her, "and it's all scribbly."

"Then read it to me," Daisy insisted. "I'm not about to fail just because I can't read your crappy handwriting."

"Maybe you should've taken your own notes," Ariella shot back, dodging someone in the hall. "You'd only have to decipher your own crappy handwriting." She took off her backpack and began looking for her notebook. "Be quick, Dais. I'm pretty sure the bell is about to…" Her voice trailed off as the warning bell sounded over the comms.

"Better get cracking," Daisy said. "We'd need a machine to translate that handwriting anyway."

"In the winter of the fourth year of the war," Ariella recited, squinting at the paper. "Or was it the third year?"

"It's the fourth year, you idiot!" Daisy said loudly. "And keep reading. We only have like eight minutes left!"

Ariella cleared her throat and said, "The newly formed country, which called itself the Raghunathan Collective Society, also known as the RCS, was attacked."

"It was by the Blackwood People's Republic, the BPR, right?" Daisy interrupted. "They were trying to eliminate any new countries that could be a threat."

Ariella shrugged. "My notes don't say, but I think you're right."

"Keep going," Daisy prodded, stepping around a kid who was sitting in the hall.

"The BPR made the first move on us, using their then superior bombs to break the new RCS to pieces." Ariella held her paper up in the light, a large line making its way through the paper. "I think I fell asleep at this part." Her eyes grazed over the big line the pencil had made, looking for the next sign of words. "It lasted for a decade." She paused. "Or maybe two?"

"I'm pretty sure that wars don't last over a decade," Daisy said, snatching the paper from her friend, attempting to read it herself. "Never mind. Guess you're right."

Ariella pumped her fist and gave her friend a triumphant look. "I told you!" She opened the door to the bathroom. "Let's finish studying here."

Daisy dropped her stuff to the floor and sat on the sink's edge. "All you know is that the RCS was created a while ago and was bombed for over ten years?"

Ariella flipped the page. "It also says that we basically dispersed for a while before the Bomb. That's when we finally became who we are today."

"And how long did that take?" Daisy asked.

"More than fifty years." She stopped to look for the spot she was at. "It took a long time just trying to recover from the BPR decimating us."

"I just thought of something," Daisy told her, adding another layer of lip gloss. "Did people just starve to death? How did we make food on the bombed land?"

"Do you seriously think we still live on top of the destroyed land?" Ariella asked incredulously. "We moved. The original RCS was destroyed by antimatter. We had to flee the scene after dropping the Bomb because it was so powerful."

Daisy gave her a dirty look before touching up her mascara in the mirror. "Do my eyelashes look too long?"

Ariella gave the mirror a quick glance. "You look like you, I guess, but with no eye shadow." She looked at the real Daisy that wasn't in the mirror. "Why no eyeshadow? I liked the green yesterday."

"I was running late and had to get JJ ready for school." She made a face of disgust into the mirror. "Pretty sure Mom was a little…" She made a drinking motion with her hands, thumb tilted toward her lips. "Ya know."

Ariella gave her a sympathetic look. "That sucks."

Daisy transformed her face into a half smile, setting her braids into a side part. "Meh, she's just fallen back down the hole." She tilted her head. "Should I leave it like this or keep it in the middle?"

"Middle," Ariella said instinctively, checking the time on her phone. "And do it quick. We barely have two minutes."

Daisy leaped off the sink and tossed her bag over one shoulder, hands flying to adjust her hair part. "Let's go and flunk this test together!"

They high-fived and laughed hopelessly, ready for failure. When they arrived in the classroom, lo and behold, Ms. Schwartz wasn't there. In her place was an old, shriveled man with a beard down to the middle of his chest. He was hunched over her desk, tapping desperately on the computer.

"Is he okay?" Ariella asked as she took her seat.

Her classmate, Connor, was holding back visible laughter. "He's been like this for the past five minutes. One of the suck-ups tried to help him, but he apparently knows what he's doing."

Ariella snickered, and the old man let out a yell of frustration. He picked up the computer and dropped it back down on the desk. "We are not doing that," he said.

The bell rang, and everyone pulled themselves out of their chairs, left hand placed near their heart. The broken screen of the computer flickered to life, playing a large projection in the air near the front desks. "All rise for your queen," the projection demanded. "All rise for the Raghunathan Collective Society, the RCS."

The old man rose out of his chair slowly, gnarled fist proudly resting on his chest. The woman in the projection, the queen, placed her own hand on top of her heart, a triangular ring glinting in the light. "I hereby pledge to forever and always."

"I hereby pledge to forever and always," the class repeated, all in sync.

"Devote all my support," she went on. The scene in the projection changed to their flag waving in the breeze. The gold triangle and paw print on it contrasted beautifully with the ebony color of the flag.

"Devote all my support." Nobody's voice wavered, all united.

"To our mighty leader." The projection went back to the queen's face, the flag fading slowly.

"To our mighty leader." Every word was said louder and louder, each one building in importance.

"Queen Rajikumari Raghunathan the Third." The name hissed around in the queen's lips like a snake.

Nobody faltered, the pronunciation having been etched into their memory since they could speak. "*Queen Ra-jee-koo-mar-ee Ra-hoo-na-thawn the Third.*"

She smiled at them as if she could see their faces through the video. "Meus es in aeternum." Her left hand joined her right to make a triangle over the symbolic RCS pin on her heart. "RCS forever."

They all copied her hands, thirty-six triangles spread throughout the room. "RCS forever." The screen went dark, and Ariella saw that it had cracks from being dropped. Their substitute teacher looked at it and made some kind of grimace. "Your teacher left the tests on this stupid online program." He smiled a cavity-stricken grin. They could all imagine a lightbulb popping over his head. "But it accidentally fell on the floor."

A kid in the back raised his hand. "But, sir," he began. "You dropped it on the desk."

"That's not what you all are going to tell her. I'm not about to lose my job over some crappy technology!" he exclaimed, fist pointed toward the ceiling. He then grabbed a piece of chalk from the board and began writing on it. "My name is Mr. Gramali." Those words were scrawled in his chicken scratch onto the board. "And today, we are going to learn about the beginning of the RCS." He stopped writing and pressed a wiry hand to his chest. "I was around then, you know." His voice was full of pride. "I was a real soldier for the RCS then."

Ariella and Connor shared a look, trying not to burst out laughing at his clearly fabricated story. "But Mr. Galamari," a boy protested. Taaj was his name, Ariella remembered. "That war was hundreds of—"

"My name is Mr. Gramali," the spindly old man corrected. "I'm not a fried octopus." He turned back to the board, engrossed in writing something. The class waited, silence choking the room to death. He soon came to a halt, the white chalk now just powder in his palm. "Where does your teacher keep the rest of the chalk?"

Taaj's hand shot up in the air, ready to be called on. Mr. Gramali cast his eyes around the room, pleading for anyone else to raise their hand. Nobody did. "Yes?" he asked, the wind taken from his sails.

"Our teacher doesn't use chalk," Taaj answered, lowering his hand back to the desk. Ariella heard him muttering something about the sub being clinically insane.

"Well, unless my eyes aren't working properly," his hand gestured to the writing on the chalkboard, "that looks like chalk to me."

Taaj's eyes narrowed slightly, pissed at having been proven wrong. "I know for a fact she doesn't use chalk on a daily basis." He turned to Daisy. "Right, Daisy?"

She only smiled weakly and shrugged. "To each their own."

Mr. Gramali clapped his hands together, stopping the conversation. "Well, I got the majority of the message down." He pointed at some of the chalk scrawls. "As you can clearly see here, we are working on a different class project today."

Ariella tried to see whatever words he thought he'd written, but she failed. Keeping her eyes on the chalkboard, she whispered to Connor, "I think Taaj might be right." Mr. Gramali turned around for a second, eyes glazing off into nothingness. She waited till he turned around before saying, "This guy has a couple of screws loose."

Connor tsked. "I think the screws are all he's got."

Ariella couldn't help but snort at that, making their substitute teacher pause in whatever he was saying. "Something funny about making 3D dioramas?" he asked. "Or is it something else?"

"3D dioramas?" she asked, but he took that as her answering the question.

"This new generation," he mumbled to himself, "thinks everything old folks say is baloney." He turned to the class, sighing. "Well, since explaining the directions for this project isn't useful to some of you, just grab the supplies and get cracking."

Ariella raised her hand sheepishly. "Mr. Gramali, what exactly are we making a diorama of?"

He gave her a bemused look before scoffing, "Figure it out yourself since you think my project is just bonkers."

Ariella looked at Connor, the corners of his mouth fighting to stay level. "Do you have any clue what we're doing?"

"Why would I know?" He got up to grab a cardboard box.

Ariella took a glance around the classroom, taking in the fact that everyone was up and out of their seats. There was one group crowded around Taaj, waiting for him to hand out scissors. Most people were scattered aimlessly around the classroom, not quite sure what they were supposed to be doing. Something clapped Ariella on the shoulders, making her jump up. She turned her head upwards, looking Daisy in the eye.

"Wanna partner up?"

"Are there partners?" Ariella asked, wondering how much Mr. Gramali had gone over in a short amount of time.

"I mean, he basically said make something 3D that was around during the war and cut us loose," Daisy said, tossing a tube of paint onto Ariella's desk.

"I thought we were making a diorama, not just a 3D object," Ariella said, twisting a loose curl around her finger.

"I highly doubt any high schooler in their right mind knows what a diorama is." Daisy sat on top of Connor's desk and picked up a pair of scissors.

Ariella pulled out her notebook, looking for ideas. Daisy slammed it shut with the palm of her hand. "Don't worry about that stuff." She smiled and held up the scissors. "I've got something." She slid toward the left side of the desk, Connor's pencil dropping to the ground with a thud. Her hand pointed the scissors at the carving on the desk, brushing across it lightly.

Ariella reached out to touch it, fingernail tracing the triangle. "Our symbol?" she asked, slightly confused. "I thought we needed some random objects from the war. Like something you can hold."

Daisy closed the scissors around her braid, a piece of green hair floating to the floor. "But isn't that what everyone else is doing? The symbol was created during the war to help unite us."

Ariella bit her lip, taking in the triangle with the paw print on the inside. Her finger went to feel the ridges and bumps along the paw print. "We unsheathed the claws," she muttered. "Took it back from them."

Daisy leaped up from the desk as Connor tried to sit back down. "Exactly! It represents rebellion. They made it to taunt us, but we took it back!"

"We took what back?" Connor asked, reaching for his pencil on the floor.

"Daisy was just giving me a history lesson," Ariella explained, removing her hand from the symbol.

Daisy moved to sit on the edge of Ariella's own desk. "We're making a 3D version of the RCS symbol because it was created during the war." She moved to grab a strand of Ariella's hair, scissors ready to snip.

"I'd rather keep my hair growing." Ariella gave her a dirty look, snatching it back. "I also don't trust you with haircuts."

"So…" Connor looked between them. "Are we making the flag or just the symbol on a piece of paper?"

"Who said you're in our group?" Daisy asked, scissors pointed towards him.

Ariella rolled her eyes. "Loosen up, Dais. He actually does his work."

"Well, he said 3D, so I assume we can't do the flag."

"We could ask to use the 3D printer," Connor suggested, eyebrows crawling together conspiratorially. "And go roam around a little too."

Ariella clapped her hands together, making Daisy jump off the desk. "Wait, that's good! We'll have a chance to escape and no homework." She walked up to Mr. Gramali with Daisy and Connor on either side of her. "Sir," her voice had the lilt of a child asking for candy. "May we go to the printing room? We need something for our project."

He narrowed his eyes. "And what exactly do you need?"

"We're making a 3D version of our symbol, sir," Daisy said, picking up the same tone Ariella used. "We want to make it perfect."

He smiled, and they saw his eyes get misty. "You kids are alright," his head shook slowly. "I have hope for you all now."

They darted out the door. Ariella did a spin around the hallway, arms stretched in glee. "Thank Raji we got out." Her hand whipped around, hitting a girl in the face. The girl curled her lip, her stormy gray eyes burning lasers into Ariella.

"Oh." Ariella's voice sounded very small. "I swear I didn't mean to—"

The girl scoffed. "Then watch where you place your hands." She stormed down the hall, leaving a red-faced Ariella in her wake.

"That was awkward," Connor said, starting down the hall again.

CARMEN SCOFFED, LOOKING OVER HER shoulder at the girl who'd just spun into her. The girl was hunched over now, whispering something to her friends. Carmen could tell she was still carrying the shame from what she'd just done. It wasn't like Carmen was still mad at the girl. It just annoyed her when people were so happy-go-lucky that they had no respect for others. She fingered a piece of hair, twisting the curl round and round as she walked back to the library.

"Hey, Carmen!" someone called to her, waving his hand wildly in the air. "What up?"

She gave him a sideways glance. "Hey, Jack. What class you in right now?"

"Math. I have a test." He shuddered and stopped in the hallway. Carmen took that as a sign that she'd be forced to listen to his rambling. "I told Mr. Moss I had a bloody nose."

She only shook her head, a smirk spreading across her face. Looking at the limp piece of tissue hanging out of his nose, she said, "And he believed it?"

"When you've got a ketchup stain on a tissue in your nose, it looks pretty believable." Jack gave her a knowing look. "Good thing he didn't ask to sniff it."

"Yep," a small chuckle escaped Carmen's mouth. "That's the most likely thing he'd ask a student after they tell him they're bleeding out."

He raised his hands in surrender. "I said it was a good thing! No need to judge me."

Carmen's eyes looked at the limp shreds poking inside his nostrils. "Whatever floats your boat." Her hand patted the top of his head. "I gotta get back to being a TA. Don't need Ms. Wilki up my ass."

Jack let out a gust of air from his lungs. "Ms. Wilki doesn't give a shit, and you know it." He paused. "I think you just want an excuse to get away from me."

Carmen made a tsking sound as she began to walk off. "Was that not obvious?"

"Someone's in a sour mood!" Jack called down toward her, legs striding to catch up. "Who upset Ms. Queen Bee today?"

"What makes you think someone upset me?" Carmen countered, legs taking longer strides as he began to catch up. Jack gave her a look, eyebrow raised to the roof. "Mr. Moss made me come in early today," she told him, taking out her lip gloss and applying another coat. "I had to take last week's test, and I have to take the one you just took after I have lunch."

He winced. "Speaking of, where were you last week? Lizzie was blowing up my phone because you promised her the notes."

Carmen angled her face at a poster on the opposite wall. *DO YOU THINK YOU'RE SPECIAL? THEN COME PERFORM AT OUR SCHOOL TALENT SHOW!* She almost snorted at the words. Who'd be dumb enough to sign up for that?

"Carmen?" She turned her head ever so slightly in his direction. He went on, "So where were you?"

"At my grandparents' house," she told him, fingering her purple and blue beaded bracelet charm. "My grandpa had a big fall, and Gram needed help taking care of him."

Jack wasn't so easily convinced. "Why couldn't one of your parents have gone? The fall was that bad?"

Carmen took the easy way out. "Yep."

He waited for her to elaborate and fill the silence, but she didn't, enjoying the awkwardness. They both walked together for a minute or two before Jack spoke up again. "Didn't we just pass the library?"

"And?"

"And weren't you supposed to get back in to talk shit with Lizzie?" Jack asked.

Carmen slowed down her walk and looked at him. "You know as well as anyone that it was an excuse." A mischievous twinkle shone in her gray eyes. "Speaking of talking shit, how's everything going with you know who?"

Jack ran a hand through his hair and sighed. "Nowhere. She's mad about me still being tight with you and Lizzie, but we aren't even dating yet."

"She controlling much?" Carmen asked, one perfectly penciled brow arched at him. "Also, don't flatter yourself. We aren't that close."

Jack placed his fist into his chest with a groan. "Brutal stab, Carmen. I'll go home and cry into my pillow tonight."

"Oh please." Her mouth twitched into a smug smile. "But seriously, is it going downhill?"

"Well, if you consider her taking a couple of hours to give one word answers, then yeah." He glared at Carmen's snicker. "Okay! How's everything going with Cooper?"

Her snicker turned into a cough. "Carry on with the rant."

"Thought so." Those words were said with such smugness that Carmen thought about shoving him into the nearby trash can. Unfortunately, he would probably have the upper hand because her combat boots had soles that were at least two and a half inches tall (maybe taller). Unlike the babes in the movies, she was a clumsy oaf when she ran in those shoes. She looked at the bottom of them, trying to mentally measure the exact length of her soles. Jack snapped his fingers in her face, and she broke her gaze away from her boots. "I was talking about my situationship," Jack told her.

Carmen focused her eyes on him, making her face seem like she was listening to his girl problems. Unfortunately, she'd seen him run through girls like nobody's business for too long. What was supposed to be different about this one?

"...And I asked about homework, but she hasn't responded yet. Do I text again or just wait?" He took out his phone, ready to type another message.

Carmen snatched it from him. "Do you seriously want to come off as the soccer fiend who's secretly the needy bitch?"

Jack gave her an annoyed glance. "I think you're the only one who's called guys bitches."

She only shrugged in return, ignoring his last statement. "She'll come around if you ignore her for a little while. It'll drive her crazy."

"But why would I want to make her crazy?" He looked around before whispering, "She scares me."

Carmen almost choked on the air in her lungs from the confession. "It's not funny!" he whined, mistaking Carmen's reaction for a laugh. "You should try fighting with her in person."

She whistled through her teeth. "Isn't she like taller than you?"

"I'm actually taller by three inches. She just likes a high…" He clicked his tongue in annoyance. "What's that thing called?"

Carmen's boots made a comfortable filler in the silence as she watched him gather his hair towards the back of his neck. "High heels?" she tried.

"No offense, but I think you're the only person who wears heels to school." Jack shook the mop of hair in his hands. "What's the thing called when you put your hair up?"

"Oh, that's a—"

A door suddenly opened behind them. Jack and Carmen scrambled away, and Carmen almost stumbled into the wall thanks to her fast maneuvering. When she glanced behind her, she saw that damned trio make their way in her direction. The girl who'd been spinning around like a top covered her mouth and began whispering to her friend with the green braids. She cast them a smirk before heading away in Jack's direction.

Jack was leaning against the wall, looking like the seniors who tried to look cool for their soccer pictures. "Good Raji," she told him, shielding her eyes. "No wonder this poor girl wants to dump you."

"Well, I for one think I look suave like this," he told her, running a hand through his hair. "Don't you?"

Carmen fake-gagged at him, hands wrapped around her throat. "I always wondered why you never have long-term relationships."

"Well, excuse me!" His eyebrows raised in a challenge. "Who's had more partners?"

She pressed a finger to the side of her face, thinking for a moment. "Including middle school?"

"Middle school relationships aren't real. They last ten days at most," Jack countered.

She scoffed, using her hand to move her hair over her shoulder. "Then what do you call the failed fling with Ms. Control Freak? You started talking last Thursday!"

A loud sigh was heard throughout the hall, seemingly echoing off the walls. "It's been on and off for a while now. You know that. We just…" He paused and twisted his finger around his hoodie string. "Keep falling apart."

"Like a dysfunctional puzzle," Carmen deadpanned. "You know it can't be solved, but you're addicted to trying."

Jack snapped his fingers. "Bingo!"

"She's a good person to keep playing this puzzle with you." She waited for Jack to take the bait.

He did. "And that means?"

"That means she's hot," Carmen explained slowly, annoyed that she had to spell it out. "I see why you keep going back."

Jack puffed out his chest indignantly. "She's the one who comes crawling back, mind you. I just—"

"Beg at her knees and swear to eat dirt if she'll take you back?" Carmen shot back.

"Whose side are you on again?"

She couldn't care less about Jack and his exploits, but she supposed it was correct to pick his side. He would unleash Lizzie on her otherwise, and that was a headache Carmen would pay to avoid. "Yours, I guess." She pulled out her phone, and it told her she'd been out for over fifteen minutes. "Seriously, Ms. Wilki is going to murder me." Jack peered at her phone on his tiptoes, leaning over her shoulder. He lost his balance and fell onto her, making Carmen crumble to her knees.

"Better hope your babe doesn't see you on top of another girl," she couldn't help but say as Jack pulled himself up. "That sounds like an argument worth watching."

"I think you'll be just fine pulling yourself up," Jack said, leaving her on the floor.

Carmen rolled her eyes and used the support of the wall to drag herself up. She used her head to gesture at the library coming up again on their loop. "Well, there's my stop." Jack watched her go. "Scared of Lizzie?" Carmen taunted, knowing that since Jack and Control Freak were back on, he and Lizzie were off.

He shivered as if a draft of wind had blown on him. "Ask her if she ate the apology chocolates. If not, I just wasted about half my paycheck on those."

"She may or may not have told me about how she flushed your apology gift down the toilet." Carmen gave him an innocent shrug. "And I may or may not have planted the idea in her head." She could tell even from twenty feet away that Jack was very unamused, so she waggled her fingers in an exaggerated goodbye before turning into the library. "Good luck on the test!"

Before she could sneak her way over to the back of the library, someone called her name. "Carmen," a very annoyed voice said, "where were you the past twenty minutes?"

Carmen flashed the teacher a gorgeous grin, not fazed by the accusatory tone. "I'm so sorry, Ms. *Lara*," she patted her stomach and winced slightly. "I just started that time of the month again. You know how it is."

Ms. Wilki bit her lip, trying to figure out how to tread the conversation. "You and I both know that it shouldn't take someone twenty minutes in the bathroom no matter what time of the month it is."

Carmen heard an additional gasp rise out of the library. "Ms. Lara, you out of all people should know how hard it is to use school tampons." She shook her head sadly, disappointed in her teacher. "I had to trek all the way to the locker rooms to get myself something usable out of my personal supply."

Lizzie appeared by Carmen's side and widened her big blue eyes at the librarian. "I really am disappointed in you, Ms. Lara." Her finger moved to wipe an invisible tear from the corner of her eye. "It's hard enough with male teachers, but you—"

Carmen took that as her chance to start up again. "You're one of us! But you're taking your power and smashing us down with it."

"Shame on you, Ms. Lara." Lizzie's voice had a quiver of sorrow as she repeated, "Shame on you."

Both girls linked arms and walked away, leaving a very embarrassed librarian in their wake. Lizzie led her friend over to their hideaway towards the back of the library and gave her a once-over. "But really, hon, where were you?"

Carmen felt Lizzie's grip tighten around her arm ever so slightly. "You know me, walking around till I drop." She tried to pry her arm away, but Lizzie grabbed her with her hand, gel extensions digging into Carmen's flesh.

"Would that include being all buddy-buddy with my ex-boyfriend?" Her voice was casual, but Carmen knew better. Lizzie looked over at her other hand as if suddenly possessed by the golden swirls on her fingers. "Not that it'd bother me."

"Liz, he's still part of the group. I'm not gonna just ice him out," she tried to say, but Lizzie was not having it.

"But he dumped me for that, that—"

"Control freak?" Carmen tried, hoping to turn her friend's anger away from herself.

It worked because Lizzie dropped her arm and clapped both hands together. "See, this is why I need you, Carmen! Who else is supposed to help come up with names for that nasty whore?"

That was not exactly what Carmen wanted to happen, but once Lizzie had an idea, she'd drag the world with her to achieve it. "All I said was that she was a control freak," Carmen clarified. "Never said anything about her being a whore." She slowly lowered herself into a beanbag.

"But you implied it," Lizzie shot back. "Because we both know it's true."

Carmen nodded, deciding that agreeing with whatever the blonde said would be easier than correcting her. "As soon as I break up with Jack, she always comes running back to him," Lizzie huffed, "like a pathetic puppy."

And just who comes running back to Jack when she breaks up with him? But Carmen kept that thought to herself and pulled out her phone. "I'm just glad I don't have to deal with being attracted to him." She shuddered at the thought. "I think I'd go positively insane."

Lizzie began convulsing with laughter, but Carmen wasn't able to tell if it was real or not. "I am not attracted to that oaf anymore! I literally threw his chocolates down the drain! Why on earth would that scream attraction?"

Carmen's gray eyes narrowed. Sometimes she wondered if something was truly wrong with Lizzie and with Control Freak. "But you were the one who planned on eating the chocolates," she reminded Lizzie. "I told you to flush them."

"Yes, and you helped make sure my attraction was squashed. I'm not going back to that idiotic fucker again!" Lizzie opened her tube of *Lobster Delight* and spread it all across her lips.

Carmen wondered if the lip gloss tasted like lobsters too. "Well, I'm glad I helped," she finally said. "It's always better to be happy than to make someone else happy."

"Exactly, hon! I'm letting go of my emotional baggage and making myself happier at the same time!" Lizzie capped her lip gloss and slid it into her cardigan. "Do you think this color brown makes me look thin?"

Carmen eyed the atrocious thing up and down. She sure wouldn't be caught dead in that. "Sure, Liz. Whatever you say."

Lizzie smiled and took out her phone. "I'm so glad we decided to be TAs at the library. It's literally like a free period!"

They both heard a bell ringing towards the front. "Damn it, you just had to jinx it, didn't you?"

Lizzie gave Carmen an innocent shrug and followed her up to where the sound of the bell was. They saw Ms. Wilki sitting in her swivel chair, pointing at a cart of books. "Take these to Mr. Johnson's class. He needs them for a project." Her eyes went to slits and landed on Carmen. "I'd prefer it if it could be done by the end of the period."

Lizzie gave their teacher a mock salute. "Will do, Ms. Lara!"

"Please, Ms. Wilki is fine by me," she corrected, hands clasped together.

Lizzie laughed, waving her hand wildly in the air. "Oh please, Ms. Wilki sounds like a grouchy old cooch whose husband divorced her." She paused and waggled her eyebrows. "Ms. Lara sounds like the young secretary who has an affair going on with her boss." She gave her teacher a wink. "I think the second one suits you best."

It took both girls all of their strength to keep straight faces while they dragged the cart out of the library, ignoring the red-faced Ms. Wilki trying to gather up a response. "See ya in a minute!" Carmen called as they strutted out the door.

Once a safe distance away, the pair began cracking up. "What the heck?" Carmen clutched her stomach while trying to push the cart. "Who in their right mind tells their teacher that they look like they're having an affair with their boss?"

Lizzie tried to mask the laughs consuming her face. "I just couldn't resist. She's way too easy to mess with."

As they made their way to the classroom, both girls continued to take turns dissolving into laughter. It wasn't until they reached the classroom door that they both took a moment to put on serious faces. Carmen turned the knob and pasted on her best smile. "Hello, Mr. Johnson." She took a look around the room and locked eyes with Control Freak. She was sure that if looks could kill, she'd be dead. Oh crap. She gestured for Lizzie not to enter the room, trying to keep a catfight from breaking out. Lizzie didn't listen.

"We're here with your books!" Lizzie finished for her cheerfully.

Mr. Johnson turned his attention away from the class and to the two of them. "Why, thank you, girls!" He made a wide sweep of the classroom with his hand. "I was just telling you about these books. Wasn't I, class?" A scatter of nods was seen across the room.

Carmen ignored the rest of his speech and grabbed Lizzie's arm. "Well, would you look at that? We need to be back before the bell rings." She smiled and waved at Mr. Johnson before dragging Lizzie out of the room with her. "Ta-ta, everyone!"

FERNANDA WATCHED AS THE BLONDE girl and her friend promptly ran out of the room. Out of all the people who had to come in, of course it had to be her. What was her name again anyway? Liana? Lisa? Lila? She couldn't care less. At least that's what she was telling herself. Good thing the girl hadn't seen her because she wasn't in the mood for a fight. Fernanda laid down on her arms and thought it over some more. Maybe she was in the mood for a fight. Sure would be better than listening to Mr. Johnson drone on and on until her ears bled. She thought about the look of shock when Lisa's (or whatever her name was) friend locked eyes with her. Fernanda honestly felt sorry for that poor girl. She was probably stuck doing Lisa's bidding.

Her friend, Aubrey, tapped her shoulder, and she realized that the teacher's talking had stopped. She raised her head slightly. "But why were we failing to defeat them?" that one annoying brainy girl from the back of the class asked, her voice barely heard over the quiet.

Fernanda zoned out again, eyes fixed on a stain on the wall. It looked like someone had puked, dipped their finger in it, and painted a perfectly round circle on the wall. She was scared to guess how long it'd been there, just taking its time to decompose on the wall. She blinked, hearing Mr. Johnson's voice on full blast now. "...But that's when the Blackwood People's Republic was stronger, Gina. That's when they had more allies and resources," Mr. Johnson said patiently. "But since then, we've always had the upper hand."

Fernanda tried to tune him out, but it was impossible. His voice got louder when he yelled at her classmates and quieter when he went back to his lecture. Beside her, Aubrey raised her hand. Fernanda could see the exasperation in her teacher's eyes as he was interrupted yet again. "What happened to all their allies?" she asked. "How did we get rid of them all?"

Mr. Johnson actually smiled. Not with his teeth of course, but it was a smile nonetheless. Fernanda thought to herself that she would rather see him frown. He could kill someone with that smile. "Very good question, Aubrey. The simple answer is nuclear weapons. They believed that they could overpower us with sheer numbers and aerial assault, but no!" His eyes lit up as he went on, rattling with the excitement of a little child. "We had more advanced weapons we had been brewing and caught them off guard."

He walked down the desks, holding his mug of coffee in his hand as he moved. Stopping at a desk where a kid was sleeping, Mr. Johnson said, "We had better tech advancements, such as the creation of the invisible electromagnetic shield to stop the effectiveness of their assaults in the air, which we still have up today." He stopped for dramatic effect as if the students were actually paying attention. "When we finally struck back, it was devastating. Sure, they had nuclear bombs, but that's when we finally had our breakthrough, taking this war to the next level." He tilted his head, like he was waiting for someone to answer. Nobody did. Everyone was looking at the walls or the ceiling to avoid his gaze. Mr. Johnson plowed on, talking like a crowd of a thousand was hanging onto his every word instead of a barely listening gang of teenagers. "We became the first civilization to learn how to manipulate antimatter. The Bomb was all it took to take them and their allies down." He snapped his fingers with his free hand. "Just like that."

Mr. Johnson looked at the desk of the sleeping student with a glimpse of malice in his eyes. Fernanda suddenly felt very sorry for whatever surprise they were about to wake up to. He slammed one hand against the side of his cup, sloshing coffee just outside of the rim. "That's what a nuclear bomb is like." Looking down at the desk with a smirk, he dropped the cup of lukewarm coffee on the desk, liquid and dried clay flying everywhere. The poor student flew awake, looking at the mess upon his desk. "And that, class, is what an antimatter bomb would look like in comparison."

The student glared at him before yawning and laying his head back down on the wet desk, moving the broken cup out of the way. "Now, before we leave, each of you grab a book. Those two girls left and—"

The bell rang, and all 28 students were up and out of their chairs before he could blink. All of Mr. Johnson's bravado was gone, and he went to his desk, hiding behind the pile of papers he was never going to grade.

Fernanda grabbed a book for both her and Aubrey before feeling her phone buzz. Sighing, she wished she had three hands to see what it said. She reminded herself that *he* had moved on. Fernanda handed Aubrey the book. "Here, I'll meet you at our table. Just give me a sec, okay?" Her phone felt like a ten-pound weight in her back pocket. She felt her friend's suspicious glance on her before she walked away.

"I'd better see you at lunch. No walking around with *him*."

"You'll see me. I promise." She waited till Aubrey was out of sight before pulling her phone out, more than ninety percent sure who had texted her. Fernanda wasn't sure she wanted to answer him.

jackj2780: hey, what's up?

Adults found it annoying that everyone communicated on one collective app, especially because you were required to add numbers to your name since lots of people had the same name, but Fernanda quite liked the futuristic feel it gave their names. It was something that separated them from the previous generation. But that wasn't the point. The point was that he was talking to her now. He couldn't score a blonde bitch, so he wanted to get the next best option: her. That's what she was anyway. To him at least. Leave him on read, her inner voice chanted. Let him try and comprehend what happened. But she couldn't be that evil. Not to him at least.

fernandaL16: nthng

fernandaL16: wbu

Three dots. Fernanda waited, curious for the response. Not that it mattered anyway. She was just doing this as a formality. She smiled, liking the way that last word in her text put a self-built wall between the two of them.

jackj2780: yea same

She scoffed and rolled her eyes. He was just about the driest texter she'd ever seen, only occasionally using a heart emoji that meant absolutely nothing at all.

Mr. Johnson cleared his throat, making her jump slightly in surprise. "Do you need something?" Which was code for I'm-on-my-break-can-you-please-leave-now. "The bell rang a few minutes ago."

"I'll only be another second, okay?" Fernanda answered, not ready to go to Aubrey.

Mr. Johnson sighed and unwrapped his black bean burrito, defeated. Who in their right mind would willingly eat a plain black bean burrito? And yet, Fernanda was unable to make out any other toppings besides the glumps of black beans. She realized that he hadn't even drained out the bean juice when she saw blackish-purple liquid dripping out of the burrito.

"Do you want a bite?" he asked drily, obviously annoyed to have an audience while he ate.

She smiled and shook her head, looking down at her phone as it buzzed with a new message.

jackj2780: you have track in two weeks right

Her smile disappeared. It was like he was a magician, able to make her moods swing without a second thought. Oh boy, here he goes again. Acting like he actually wanted to see her. But she was just his second option, the side girl.

fernandaL16: yea why

Fernanda wondered why she was texting him. The thought disappeared as soon as she saw the three dots again, curiosity turning to anger because shit, he was really gonna try this again.

jackj2780: what events

Fernanda considered leaving him on read and deleting the conversation, but she decided against it. No need to burn a bridge…yet. She sighed deeply as she let her fingers fly along the electronic keyboard.

fernandaL16: 800

Aubrey probably thought she'd lost her resolve and given in because of how long this had taken. Keeping her eyes on her phone, Fernanda swung her backpack and waved goodbye to Mr. Johnson. She could swear she heard him give a sigh of relief, but she probably just imagined it. "See you Thursday."

jackj2780: Just one event this time huh

Fernanda hated how easily he still got under her skin. How dare he try to undermine her achievements! It wasn't like he was some champion on his soccer team, stuck in that middle spot between JV and varsity. He always thought he was on top of the world. She took a deep breath and replied as kindly as possible.

fernandaL16: dude, it's a varsity meet

fernandaL16: only the best schools in the entire rcs are invited

She looked up just in time to avoid walking into someone. They sighed and moved out of her way, muttering something about phone-addicted teenagers, though she was pretty sure they were a teen themselves. Feeling her phone buzz, she immediately looked down again.

jackj2780: nice

She felt surprisingly deflated about his nonchalant reply and decided to wait and see if he gave more of a response. Not that she actually cared.

jackj2780: did you do the homework

fernandaL16: what homework

Fernanda could make an educated guess on what he was referring to but decided she wanted to make him explain since he showed her that explaining was a weakness of his.

jackj2780: the math homework

fernandaL16: yea finished it a while ago

Fernanda sighed and rolled her eyes, stopping in the middle of the hall.

fernandaL16: ill send it

fernandaL16: *One Document Sent*

Her brain screamed at why she was still nice to him. Why did she still care? She couldn't give herself a good reason as she began walking again. It wasn't like he would ever need her again.

jackj2780: k

jackj2780: did you do it all

Fernanda almost rolled her eyes. Why ask her when he could just look at the document that she graciously sent? She looked up from her phone and saw that she was almost at the cafeteria.

fernandaL16: nope, did most of it tho

jackj2780: r u able to explain in person

If he asked her to come with him one more time, she might just have to go up to him and rip off his lips. One of your more preferred features that he has, her brain teased back, her brain teased back, tired of being ignored. She sighed deeply and sat down at her lunch table, glancing discreetly over to his table before answering.

fernandaL16: i already texted it just take a look at it

jackj2780: thank you

Glad to know his mom taught him some damn manners. As Fernanda finished texting, Aubrey looked up at her, surprise written all over her face. "Wow, nice to see you."

She smiled. "Are you that surprised to see me?" Fernanda already knew the answer but had some satisfaction in asking her.

"Sorta. I mean, I didn't think you had it in you," Aubrey said honestly. "He's done stuff like this before, and you ignored it." She paused. "But you're strong, and I knew you'd cut the crap soon."

Even though what Aubrey said was true, it still hurt. It suddenly became harder to keep her lips turning upward as she said, "I made a promise to you, and I'll keep it." She put her phone on silent, refusing to check her phone until lunch was over.

"Wanna walk around once we finish eating?" Aubrey asked. "I don't think I have it in me to sit still for another thirty minutes."

Fernanda took out her rice bowl and shrugged. "Don't see why not. As long as we don't have to be anywhere near that area." She made a vague but useful gesture toward Jack's direction. Out of the corner of her eye, she saw Jack looking at her, his frown evident. It made the fake smile on her face turn real. Guess he did feel something. And that was enough. For now at least.

Aubrey cleared her throat. "Don't think about that asshole. You deserve so much better."

Fernanda put a large bite of rice and chicken in her mouth. "Yeah, kinda hard to tell yourself that over and over when you don't believe it," she muttered through food.

Aubrey didn't hear her. She was scrolling through something on her phone while eating her burrito.

Fernanda sighed and put the lid on her container of rice. "Bri, let's go walk around. I don't wanna sit still right now."

Aubrey sighed and looked up from her burrito. "I'll walk and eat just this once." She placed her phone in her pocket and got up, following close behind her friend.

Fernanda leaped up, spinning around on her toes as they escaped the claws of the lunchroom. "Let's go!" She hopped back to link her arms with Aubrey.

Aubrey shook her head, pretending to be annoyed but secretly smiling. "Slow down. I wanna finish this."

Fernanda let go of her arm and wrinkled her nose in disgust. "You're just like Mr. Johnson, wanting to sit alone and eat your wet black bean burrito."

Aubrey gave her a look of confusion. "Since when does Mr. Johnson eat black bean burritos?" She paused a second to finish chewing before saying, "Also, this is way more than black beans. I'm not that boring!"

Fernanda shook her head dismally. "You made him start on a ten-minute-long tirade about antimatter. He just kept going on and on about it, like it's some new invention or something!"

"But it was huge, Fernanda! It was the first time we created something that wiped out half of humanity," she said seriously.

Fernanda sighed and linked her arm back through Aubrey's. "Yeah, yeah. But it was to make the RCS a safer place. It'd be crazy to think that there was another option to protect ourselves if we didn't use the Bomb."

Aubrey thought for a moment before agreeing. "Yeah, I just wonder about the what-ifs sometimes. And how we even figured out how to take that leap." Aubrey shook her head in amazement. "We really have come a long way."

Fernanda began skipping, dragging her friend along too. "Forget about school. Let's go have some fun!"

"In school?" Aubrey asked, ignoring the looks they got from a group of girls.

"We'll make our own fun," Fernanda said defiantly. "Come on!

"Isn't that the girl Lizzie was talking about?" Christine whispered to Taylor, eyes on her high ponytail. "I swear she said that she has a high ponytail."

Taylor nodded. "I think you're right, Chris. Isn't she friends with the redhead?"

"I think so," Christine began, walking away from the direction that the high ponytail girl and her friend went. "I remember Lizzie calling me about how Jack sent her the breakup gift."

Taylor ran a hand through her magenta-streaked hair. "Really?" Her fingers stopped at the split ends. "Lizzie told me that she broke up with Jack, and then he went running to High Ponytail Girl."

A third girl forced herself in between the two, linking arms through them both. "Well, Carmen texted me that Jack told her that he was on his knees for High Ponytail Girl. He was completely enamored!" Christine and Taylor both made a face at the mention of that particular person.

Taylor unlinked her arm from Kate and gave her a sideways glance. "Um, Jack likes Lizzie. It's High Ponytail Girl who's literally throwing herself at Jack, so he has no choice but to break up with Lizzie."

"I guess that'd make sense as to why he spent so much on their breakup gift." Christine shook her head solemnly. "Because he wants to keep her around."

Kate dropped Christine's arm to pat her silky black hair. She would have to tell Kate how much she disliked that some other time. "Did you ever think it might be just because he's got a shit ton of money?" Kate's voice dropped to a conspiratorial whisper. "I heard that Carmen told Lizzie to flush it down the toilet."

Taylor groaned in frustration. "I hate all these people making up this stupid-ass gossip. We all know Lizzie would never let Jack break up with her."

Christine and Kate shared a knowing look before Christine spoke up, careful not to trigger the pink-haired landmine. "Yeah." She bit her lip for a second, trying to find the right words. "But then why would Lizzie have gotten the breakup gift?"

"Do you really think he sent her a breakup gift?" Taylor began indignantly, pointer finger moving side to side like a pendulum. "That was his expression of his love, but Lizzie was just so fed up with him that she flushed it down the toilet."

Kate rolled her eyes at Taylor's insistence. "Give me a break! Lizzie's just jealous that Jack's willing to eat shit to stay with High Ponytail Girl."

Christine decided to say something before Taylor could go on another pro-Lizzie tirade. Not that she didn't like Lizzie, but everyone had their limit. "I think I speak for all of us when I say this. Jack wouldn't eat shit to keep his own mom alive."

Taylor seemed to like that, bobbing her head at Christine's words. "Exactly, so Lizzie was just letting go of the dead weight and moving on with this chapter of her life." She fingered the obsidian hoop in her ear. "Since High Ponytail Girl was already foaming at the mouth for him, he felt like he had to go to her."

"Then explain why Carmen told me that Jack told her that High Ponytail Girl was dumping him," Kate shot back, voice rising louder. "Jack's actually desperate for her!"

If covering her ears wouldn't offend the girl, Christine would've done it in a heartbeat, but her ears suffered from the pitch Taylor's voice rose to. "Carmen's such a lying bitch. She was also the one who told you that Taaj liked you as a joke." When Kate's face crumbled slightly, the magenta-headed bomb said, "Yeah, so I'm not sure I'd believe her when she says Jack's about to eat dirt for the girl."

Christine stepped in between them and pointed at an upcoming door, not wanting to talk about Lizzie or Jack or especially Carmen anymore. "Looks like James's room is coming up. Let's go in early."

"It's Mr. Smith," Taylor reminded her, annoyed. "Just because he's your brother-in-law doesn't mean you get to call him by his first name."

Christine shot her a perfect smile, opening the door and letting them in. "You're just mad he failed your last project."

For once, Taylor had nothing to say. Kate held up a fist for Christine behind Taylor's back. Christine bumped it before taking a seat towards the back of the class.

James looked up from his phone and got up from his chair. "Ready for today's lesson?"

Kate placed her feet up on her desk. "And what might today's lesson be about, Mr. Smith?"

He eyed her gigantic sneakers that took up more than half the desk. "We're actually putting our theories to the test. Make as big a mess as you can and take notes. You're graded on the proficiency of the notes you take." He grabbed Taylor's phone and placed it in his pocket. "This may be a group project, but you each need your own notes."

Christine rolled her eyes and slumped into the desk between her two friends. "What if you just give us all passing grades, and we won't bother you the whole class?"

James patted his younger sister-in-law on the head, messing up her jet black hair. She'd have to tell him sometime how much she hated that. "What if you do your work, and I'll decide not to fail your group."

Christine laid her head on the desk to move away from his hand. "Shouldn't you be getting the stuff out for us to explode? We need a lot of stuff for our project."

He shook his head at them all. "I *was* going to tell you all to do it outside." He bent his knees as if to tell them all a secret. "But if everyone destroys the classroom, I get the class next to the greenhouse."

Taylor's eyes widened. "You mean the one with the sunroof?"

"The very one." James made a wide sweep around the room. "Please destroy this room to your heart's desire."

Taylor wove a hand through her magenta and black locks. "On one condition."

He narrowed his eyes at her. "And what might that be?"

Taylor's deep brown eyes were sharp as glass as she eyed him. "You give us all A's without making us take notes."

Christine lifted her head up, ebony hair bouncing from the movement. "Or we'll go tell the principal that you want to endanger students." She shrugged innocently. "Your choice."

He gave them all a nasty look, walking back toward his desk as the students started pouring in. "Good one."

All three girls shared a smug look. Taylor's hand went for her phone before groaning, "Of course I forgot that part of the deal. My phone!"

Kate shook her head disgustedly. "Taking notes isn't even that bad. There really was no need for all that threatening."

"Well, now it's less work." Christine pulled out her own phone and found Carmen's number. "We have more time to slack off."

The bell rang, signaling the end of lunch and the start of class. Usually, the class would be jam-packed with students, but it seemed like not many people wanted to do the experiment today. "Welcome, students!" the girls heard James begin. "I hope you all finished your hypotheses and reading the lab procedures because we're starting our lab today."

Christine looked at Carmen's name on her phone, unsure if she should reach out or just let things be. She caught Taylor giving her phone a nasty look, but she ignored it. "Phones away," Taylor hissed loudly, as if Christine cared that Taylor forgot to ask for her phone back. "Or do you have Mr. Brother-in-Law wrapped around your finger so much that you don't even have to care?"

"Well, excuse you for projecting all your jealousy on Christine," Kate whispered at Taylor, leaning her head against the desk behind her. "Not our fault you made an idiotic mistake."

Christine looked at the last texts Carmen had sent her, letting Taylor and Kate get into yet another spat.

caRmEnoRloV1115: dont mention that shit to me again
caRmEnoRloV1115: dont even talk to me again
caRmEnoRloV1115: i mean it chrissie

Her fingers hovered on the edge of the keyboard, ready to type out an apology, but she stopped. Sure, she and Carmen had their fair share of spats, but nothing as bad as their last one. It had started as a normal sleepover, eating pasta in the kitchen and playing on Carmen's new VR gaming system. But when Christine had to use the bathroom, she saw a picture of a girl. It looked like Carmen when she was younger or maybe a cousin, so she asked about it. Carmen responded by grabbing the picture and telling her not to ask about it again. That made Christine more curious, asking if it was a secret cousin or an estranged family member. Carmen blew up, telling her to shut up and not ask again. Christine stayed over for the rest of the world's most awkward sleepover and then fled home at the crack of dawn. Afterwards, Carmen made sure to bombard her with those creepy texts.

Taylor peered over at Christine's screen, and a look of horror passed over her face. "Gimme that!" She snatched the phone and deleted the half-written "sorry" on the screen. "You are not about to apologize to that girl again, okay?" Christine had told both her friends about what happened because what else was she supposed to do?

Silence descended over the room. The whole class turned to look at the pair as if waiting for Christine's response to Taylor. The black-haired girl was pretty sure that half the kids in the class knew about her fight with Carmen. It wasn't exactly the most inconspicuous fight when it was with one of the school's most popular students.

James appeared out of thin air, grabbing the phone out of Taylor's grip. "No phones in class, missy." He placed it in his pocket and began walking back to his desk. "I'll keep this until class is over."

Kate's feet finally left her desk, and she leaned over to Christine. "Are you dead serious trying to apologize to Carmen right now?"

It was at that moment that Christine wished she could sink into the depths of the floor, away from all the questions and stares and rumors. She could feel the eyes burning into her, making the hairs on her arm crawl up and down like a spider. "Well, it's not like you stopped talking to Carmen after that." Christine's words oozed out like poison, aiming to kill their victim. They didn't even land near their target.

"You know as well as anyone our relationship is purely transactional." Kate shot back, shuddering at the thought of her and Carmen being all buddy-buddy. "She gives me gossip. I give her...more gossip."

Taylor raised a jet black brow at Kate's words. "And what gossip might you be giving her?"

Kate only leaned back in her chair, sneakers back on top of her desk. "What'll you give me in return?"

Christine gave Kate a sideways glance. "Aren't we your friends? Why does everything have a damn price?"

James clapped his hands twice from the front of the classroom. "We are now going to begin our experiments. Do not worry about the damage it may cause to the classroom. We'll be getting a new one soon." A quiet chatter sounded across the room from those words. They had heard rumors about the greenhouse room, but they were never sure. "The bigger the explosions, the better." And with that, he wheeled out a cart full of jars, bottles, and tubes. People began to crowd around the cart, making James give up on pushing it, and he stalked back to his desk. "Go wild. Just finish up by the end of the period and hand in your notes. Don't forget safety gear."

Christine got up and made her way over to the cart, grabbing the supplies they needed. She gestured for her friends to follow her. "Let's go over to the corner," she yelled over the roar of people shoving to grab the items they needed. "Nobody likes to go over there anyway. It's a tight squeeze." She handed a bottle to Taylor.

"How much are we using anyway?" Kate asked, rolling on a swivel chair she'd gotten from who knows where.

Christine grabbed all of the goggles and gloves. She tossed the gear to each of them before letting them rest on top of her head, not wanting to get the dreaded raccoon eyes. "First, we need..." Kate looked over their experiment procedure. "One cup of the pink stuff. Then, two cups of the bluish-green stuff."

"You mean the teal stuff?" Taylor corrected, goggles also on top of her head.

Kate placed her goggles on with a satisfying snap. She eyed their unprotected eyes and shook her head. "If you two go blind, then that's not my problem. I tried."

Christine rolled her eyes and placed the goggles over her eyes. "Happy now?"

"Never said I was sad about the idea," Kate clarified, pouring pink and blue liquid into their respective beakers. "But, sure. I'm happy now."

Taylor took her goggles all the way off and raised an eyebrow at Kate, tossing them onto a nearby desk. Kate ignored her, pulling on flamingo-colored rubber gloves. "Who wants to do the explosion?"

Christine looked at Taylor, who was suddenly fascinated with a classmate's yellow beaker. "I guess I'll do it." Kate handed her a pair of grass-colored rubber gloves. Christine pulled them on, struggling a little bit with the sweat she'd been building on her fingers. After the glove ordeal, she poured the blue stuff into a bowl and reached for the pink liquid. She looked at Kate, who had pulled out her phone and was recording.

"You got this!" her friend cheered from about ten feet away. "Is the explosion supposed to be big?" Christine questioned, suddenly apprehensive. "Like where I might be in the crossfire?" A loud bang from a beaker sounded from across the room, and Kate just grinned back at her, so she dumped the pink stuff into the bowl and skittered backward. She wasn't fast enough. Soapy foam began pouring and pouring and pouring. Kate moved backward too, scared of her nice sneakers getting ruined.

Other students from around the classroom noticed the spectacle, all watching wide-eyed like googly-eyed dolls. Even James looked up from behind his computer screen, which Christine was pretty sure had a phone behind it. But the explosion got bigger and bigger, the tower of foam tumbling like toy blocks. Screams rang out in the room. Twenty teens and one mid-twenties-aged man ran to stay away from the foam.

Christine looked around to find that a few students had the bright idea of sitting on the desks, and she immediately hopped on the nearest one, knocking a book and phone into the foam. The foam stopped after covering nearly half the classroom. After making sure that everyone was safe, James smiled. "This is exactly what I want." Most of the class shared confused looks, having thought that Christine was in for it now. "Just make it bigger now!"

Slowly, people began chattering again, a buzz filling the room. Christine lowered herself from the desk and headed over to the rolling cart. Kate followed suit, taking care that her shoes didn't get a speck of unicorn crap on her shoes. It wasn't long before they copied their earlier experiment and made another wave of foam, this one smaller than the first because of their dwindling resources.

Some time after their second explosion, James decided that the classroom was banged up enough to go and report. "Don't do any more experiments," he told them sternly. "All we have to do now is say that someone accidentally miscalculated their measurements, and we'll get the classroom by the greenhouse!" Cheers were heard from around the classroom, including from Christine herself. With that happy note, he left them to their own devices.

Taylor spawned behind Christine, patting her on the head. Christine would really have to explain to her another time about how much that bothered her. "Are we taking our phones back now or what?"

Christine eyed the exit door, ajar from when James had left. "We do have a couple of minutes before he gets back. James loves a good chat." They crept over to the giant sea of papers, and Christine rolled her eyes at the half-filled clear box of phones. She grabbed at the box handle and gasped when it refused to open. "He locked it."

Taylor scoffed as if the idea of Mr. Smith finally figuring out that the box could lock was preposterous, but her face soon morphed into an expression of shock when it stayed shut. "Who do you think told him? No offense, but I highly doubt he figured this out on his own."

Christine waved a hand dismissively. She examined the box more carefully. "I think it's glass so—"

"No!" Taylor interrupted, horror apparent in her voice. "Can you imagine what everyone else would think if we smashed our phones with the case? We'd be jailed for the murder of like fifteen phones!" That only left one option. "KATE!" they both screamed over the noise of the classroom. "WE NEED YOUR HELP!"

The girl slowly but surely made her way over to them, dodging the remnants of old foam explosions. "Your sneakers will be fine!" Taylor jumped up and down. "We don't know when Mr. Smith will come back."

Kate rolled her eyes and began taking lunge-like steps over any speck of foam. "I think I'd rather be safe than sorry. You never know how strong Mr. Smith's acid is." When she arrived in front of the two girls, Taylor proceeded to stuff the glass case into Kate's hands. "Someone told him that there was a lock, so we need you to open it." Kate gave the handle a harsh jerk. It opened like an attic door, slow and creaky. "Guess the lock sucks ass," she told them, chuckling. "It's kind of pitiful that you couldn't open it up."

Christine gave Kate's arms a glance. "Well, it's not like we're all martial art demons. None of us have those muscles of yours." Both girls couldn't help but be in awe (although they'd never admit it) when Kate flexed again, arms jacked up. "These things are useful for certain situations," she admitted, eyes glinting with a hint of mischief. "People love to underestimate a girl."

Taylor and Christine shared a look, trying to decide whether or not they should ask what was meant by that sentence, but before any of them could say another word, one of the guys stood on top of a desk with a box of matches on display. "Atten-TION!" They all held back a collective snort as half his matches from the box flew down to the floor. He ignored them and said, "We are doing a ginormous kaboom, and you all get to watch!" He jumped from the desk, lighting three matches at once as he landed.

"How'd he do that?" Taylor whispered, entranced.

Nobody answered. The room was waiting for him to make his next move. A vat of a white, greasy substance was brought forth by his experiment partners and placed on the desk that he'd been standing on. He waved the fiery matches around in the air before letting them drop into the vat. Unified screams rang out across the room as flames shot up towards the ceiling. "WHAT THE FUCK, CONNOR?" someone shouted out.

The boy, who Christine now knew was Connor, leaped back as if his hair was on fire. "It'll die down," he promised, his lackadaisical grin faltering. "Right, guys?"

His partners rubbed the backs of their necks. "Yeah…no."

Everyone just watched as smoke began pouring from the vat, the plastic container melting like butter. The fire was famished, devouring the wooden desks and savoring their taste. Their eyes were held captive by the flames as they grew and grew and grew. That's when the fire alarm went off. The class broke away from the fire's spell, rushing around like half-crazed cats.

Christine watched as Taylor turned back for a second to look through the box of phones. "We gotta go!" She grabbed at Taylor's arm, trying to tear her away. "It's an actual fire!"

"Geez, Christine. You might be able to let your phone burn, but not me." She grabbed her phone and broke from her friend's grasp. "We can go now."

Christine followed her out for a moment before realizing what she was leaving behind. As if still bewitched by the fire, she had a mad thought. Her parents would kill her for leaving her phone behind to burn. She let Taylor walk out of the room by herself and looked back at the fire. It wasn't extremely big, and her phone was really important. Christine shuddered at the thought of leaving it and went back for the box of phones. Heck, why not just take the whole thing? People would be pissed if she only grabbed her own cellphone, but the case was heavier than she expected, so she tripped slightly from the extra weight. The crackling sound of the fire soon consumed her hearing as she started for the door. Without taking a second glance back, she ran out the door with the box full of phones. That's when she ran smack dab into a wall of bodies. "FIRE!" she yelled as she shoved her way through, ignoring the teacher calling for her to come back. She wasn't really fond of the idea of being stuck with a slow-moving class when she could get out much quicker herself.

"Wait, is that an actual fire?"

"Is it real this time?"

"Move over. I wanna see how big it is!"

Yeah, there was a real fire. Yeah, it was big. She was also pretty sure that the booming voice yelling at them all to break away was a teacher trying to keep their ducks in a row. She snorted to herself, weaving through the now-empty halls. She recognized one of the upcoming halls and broke into a faster run, racing to the exit. It was hard to run with arms wrapped around the case of phones, but she burst through the exit door like she herself was on fire, the box moving from side to side with her.

"I heard that it was Mr. Leanore's class that started the fire. He asked them to sit down, and they set him on fire instead."

"Well, I was told that it was Ms. Wilki's library. Her TAs decided to revolt and burn down the school."

"But she told me that he said that it was Mr. Smith. He was sick of teaching, so he set the school ablaze."

The rumors swirled around Christine as she made her way through the crowd, rolling her eyes at how fast gossip began to spread. Where were her classmates? She kept going, looking around the yard. The more she moved, the more the rumors shifted.

"Hey…isn't that the girl Carmen ditched? The one who has the phones right now?"

"Wait, she's Mr. Smith's daughter! She's probably in cahoots with him. Why else would she have phones in the middle of a fire?"

"Maybe they both took revenge on Carmen together. Tied her up and burned her alive."

People really were pitiful sometimes. What did they think this was? A cult? She kept going, feet moving faster to get away from the talking. She started jogging, phones clanging chaotically the faster she went. Their words bounced around her head as she continued to make her way around the side of the school, and she willed herself to go faster.

"Christine?"

She stopped and turned towards the sound. There stood Kate, hair all out of place and shirt slightly ripped. "Kate?" She saw her friend running and trying to wrap her in a hug despite the stupid box of phones in the way. Kate broke away and gave her friend a confused look. "Why do you have the phones?" She shook her head and sighed. "Please don't tell me you went back for the phones."

Christine tried to talk, but her voice seemed to have fled. She nodded instead. "What the fuck? You know that when a school is burning, you run from it, right?"

"Yeah." Her voice sounded so far away. So scratchy and weird. "I know."

"Did Taylor put you up to it?" Kate demanded harshly. "Did she tell you to grab all the phones before the fire got there?"

"No." That was all she could get out. All her voice let her say.

"Be honest, Chrissie. You need to stop covering your friends' asses." Kate's eyes stared into her soul, reading her every thought.

"Taylor grabbed her phone," she explained with her raspy throat. "I grabbed the rest."

Kate jabbed her finger towards the school, where she could now see that part of the roof had caved in. Flashes of red and wafts of smoke rose from where a ceiling once stood. "Do you see that? Do you see how big it's gotten?"

Christine just stood there, watching the flames consuming and consuming. "Yeah."

"That could have been you." Kate's face was somehow in front of her now. "That could have been you burning alive."

Did she have to spell it out so plainly? Sure, from their vantage point, it looked like half the school was in flames, but nobody was actually in there, right? Nobody could actually die from such a silly little accident. It was just an accident. "Nobody's still inside, right?" She heard the words come out. She felt her lips form the syllables and sounds, but it didn't feel real.

"It's been five minutes, Chrissie. You tell me if that's enough time to evacuate two thousand people from a multistory building."

Something fell to the ground, making a big, loud cracking sound. But it couldn't make her tear her eyes away from the fire. Nothing could. "We don't have that many people," she protested, trying to suppress the growing panic in her head. "It can't be that bad."

"It's not that bad," Kate agreed. "It's worse."

"But it wasn't that big when I was in the classroom," she tried to say. "It wasn't even covering half of the classroom!"

Kate shrugged and looked at the school. "Guess explosions can spread fast."

But logically, it made absolutely zero sense. How did a fire spread so fast in five measly minutes?

"Pick up the phones, Chrissie. We gotta find the others."

"What phones?"

"The ones that were in the box," Kate told her.

Christine realized that she must have asked that last part aloud. She looked at the ground, shards of glass surrounding her like snow. "Where'd the box go?" she asked stupidly.

"It broke," Kate said to her, crouching down to grab the phones. "Start picking them up. Might as well save them if you went back for them."

So she did, ignoring the sharp stings of glass as she began to complete her job. Christine felt guilty now. Why was she able to go back and grab a huge case of phones while others were in there melting to death?

"We got them all," Kate said, starting to walk away. "Let's go find the rest of them."

Christine looked down at her hands, broken phone shards tinted in her scarlet drops. "Why are you here?"

"When we were all running," Kate began, sighing slowly to herself, "we didn't try and stay together, so I got separated from the pack and just scrambled to find an exit."

Christine had nothing to say to that, eyes glazing over from the smoke. She badly wanted to look at the fire and see how big it had gotten in the past couple of minutes. Or seconds. Time was confusing for her at the moment. "Where are they?" she croaked out, voice drying out.

"That's what we're doing right now," Kate told her, giving her a look. "Why would I know where they are if I got separated from them?"

That made sense, she supposed, but then again, stuff that was supposed to be black and white was getting burned alive. Weren't the firefighters supposed to rescue everyone? Wasn't the fire supposed to grow slowly? Weren't people supposed to escape and just let this become a small dot in their memory as they grew old?

"So the people inside are dying?"

"I hope so," Kate muttered. "I'd rather them die quickly from an exploding shelf than be burned alive like a marshmallow."

Like a marshmallow when you placed it in the campfire and laughed, Christine couldn't help but think. Like a marshmallow when you smashed its guts between two graham crackers and let its essence leak out onto your fingers with a grin. Like a marshmallow when you ate it, crushing it over and over and over. That's when Christine knew that she could never eat a s'more again.

She must have made some type of concerning noise because Kate turned back to look at her. "Are you okay? Too much smoke for you?"

"No."

They kept walking, feet taking them towards the main entrance, yet they were still so far away. At one point, when they stood on top of the hill overlooking the school, they could see all of the bodies gathered outside.

"Do we have to?" Christine pleaded, the words rushing out before she could think. "Do we have to see them?"

"Are you scared to see them?" Kate asked. Then, realizing her mistake, covered her mouth from her stupidity. "Oh, you're scared of who you won't see."

The thought had never even occurred to her, but she let it roam free in her brain courtesy of Kate. Christine shook her head. "Never mind, let's just get it over with." She ran away from Kate, away from the fire, and away from the marshmallows melting into gooey sugar. It was exhilarating to run down the hill. It made you want to smile and laugh and do all the things you weren't supposed to do when you abandoned dead people. But she couldn't stop when she reached the bottom because of inertia or velocity or something like that. She had to smash into someone, knocking them to the ground. Her handful of phones and her blood scattered left and right, making her curse to herself.

"I'm so sorry!" she blubbered, pulling the fallen girl up.

D*aisy grabbed the hand of* the girl who ran her over, mentally cursing the fact that Ariella must have already gone on without her. She had finally found her friend in the crowd of people after getting the go-ahead from her teacher to leave the group when the new girl bowled her over, and she lost sight of Ariella. Pasting on a smile, she turned to the girl. "Don't worry. Just be glad you got out." She shook her head, accidentally hitting the girl with her box braids. "The Black Claws are ruthless."

"Excuse me?"

The other girl looked confused, and Daisy assumed she must have been too focused on getting out to have heard the news. "We had a bomb planted in the building," Daisy explained to her. "Not antimatter or anything like that, but it blew up in the greenhouse area. The principal just made an announcement saying that it was the work of the Black Claws."

The girl looked more perplexed than ever, her nose twisting to an odd position. "But I saw the fire start," she tried to say, breaking into a coughing fit.

Daisy immediately handed her a water bottle. "I did too. A lot of the classrooms have a window that overlooks the greenhouse." She looked back at the school, eyeing the heap of what used to be a bell on the ground. Everything that had made the main entrance gorgeous lay either in heaps or in ashes around it. "The Black Claws were attempting to revolt against the queen's new laws."

"Who the fuck are the—" A loud cough, followed by Daisy slapping her on the back, interrupted the girl speaking. "Black Claws?"

"They're the pro-BPR group that's extremely fond of bombs," Daisy told her, watching as the girl took another slow sip of water. "They bombed Cliffdale High School as an act of defiance."

"But I saw the fire start."

Daisy couldn't help but be annoyed with the girl now. Hadn't she already explained everything? Kids were starting to look their way now, mouths in big round O's when they heard her say that.

"I saw some guy jump onto a desk and set a vat of oil on fire!"

Maybe the prolonged exposure to heat and smoke had done something to her head. "What's your name?" Daisy asked, trying to calm her down.

"Christine." She looked back at Daisy as if to prod her to keep talking.

"Well, Christine, I don't know what you think you saw or didn't see, but what I do know is that a bomb did indeed go off in the greenhouse, and that bomb was planted by the Black Claws." She winced slightly as Christine's expression morphed into one of confusion. Good Raji, she was about to cause a scene, wasn't she?

"I saw it happen!" She was getting hysterical now, a symptom of prolonged exposure to heat. Daisy was sure of that now. Christine turned to one of the crowd members who had gathered around them. "I ran from the fire! Ask Kate! Ask Taylor!" She turned to her side as though one of the girls she mentioned would spawn by her side. "Kate was just right there!" She waved her arms wildly, voice getting louder and louder like they all weren't listening to her ramble. "Kate was just next to me!" Christine flung the water bottle to the side in frustration.

"Maybe Kate was right by you," Daisy told her. "But if she were here, I'm sure she'd say the same thing."

That made things worse. "She was right here talking to me about the fire! She saw what I saw! The whole class saw!" She didn't stop there, her eyes wide and scary. "There was no damn bomb!"

Except that Daisy had seen the bomb explode in the greenhouse, the fire had spread from there. Christine broke through the ring of gawkers, stumbling off to perhaps find Kate. "I know what I saw. You will not tell me otherwise!"

So that went well. Daisy's first patient that she ever tried to help was completely delusional. She dusted the dirt off her knees. Now would be a good time to find Ariella, wherever her friend had gotten to. "Ariella?" she called out, parting her way through the crowd. "Where'd you go, Ariella?" Her throat began to hurt, and she realized she'd left her water bottle on the ground when Christine had flung it away. "Well, that's just great." Daisy pulled out her phone to see that she had three missed calls from her mom. She unlocked her phone with her face and tapped on her mom's number, holding the phone to her ear.

"Hello?" There was a faint rustling noise, but her mom's voice came in clearly after a moment. "Can you hear me, Flower?"

Good Raji. She hated that nickname with every fiber of her being, but now was not the time. "I can hear you just fine. I suppose you heard about the bomb?"

Her mom clicked her tongue as if dismissing the question. "Well, everyone has by now. They aren't planning on keeping you there, are they?"

Daisy's voice lost any hard edge it may have had. "No, they said that as long as you have a ride, you can leave to go home. Can you come get me and Ariella?"

Her mom sighed deeply, and Daisy could hear the eyeroll through the phone. "JJ!" she yelled to her son, who was most likely watching TV downstairs. "GET YOUR COAT ON! WE GOTTA GET DAISY!"

Daisy didn't even pull back from the bellowing sound that came from the phone, though she wanted to. "Ariella can have a ride too, right?"

"Yeah, sure. As long as you're able to watch JJ tonight while I'm out." Daisy was pretty sure her mom was applying lipstick at the moment. She could hear the telltale sound of her puckering and doing duck lips, although Daisy had told her a million times over that it wasn't necessary.

"But we just got bombed at!" She couldn't even disguise the frustration in her voice. "You're leaving me alone with JJ when we—" She stopped herself, took a deep breath, and restarted. "Yes, I will watch JJ as long as you have dinner in the fridge."

"But you can make mac and cheese," her mom said, annoyed. "We have plenty of food in the cabinets."

In. Out. Daisy controlled the air coming in and out of her nose. "Please make sure something is in the fridge when I get home," she told her calmly, malice just below the surface, "and I will watch JJ tonight." While you go out and party till vomit pours from your nose was what Daisy decided not to tack on to her sentence.

A loud, dramatic sigh filled Daisy's left ear. "Fine, I'll be there in ten." And the call ended.

"Love you too, Mom," she told the disconnected call, a small laugh breaking through as she looked for Ariella's number. She had to find Ariella in the ten minutes it took for the car to come, and as long as she answered the phone, it'd all work out. "The person you are trying to reach is—" Daisy hung up and tried again, only for it to go straight to voicemail.

Ariella hadn't gone back in, had she? Her friend wouldn't be stupid enough to try to go back in and find Connor, would she? Even though whatever flames at the front of the building were long gone, she was still worried. "Ariella probably has a crush on him," she muttered to herself as she began going toward the school against the flow of traffic. She was probably trying to do some heroic crap to save him. That's just your mind making up stories to scare you, said her more reasonable side. There's no way she actually went inside the building. But she remembered the times Ariella had dragged her into the dumbest situations. Daisy stopped. "She definitely went inside." She took a deep breath and walked towards the doors of the school, hoping that the makeshift security guard wouldn't turn their attention towards her. The bomb detonated toward the back of the school, but they were being extra cautious by not letting anyone back in. It probably was for the best, but it was still frustrating when it came to a situation like this.

"Daisy?" She paused, stopping in her tracks as the voice continued, "Why on earth are you going back inside?" Daisy turned around and almost collapsed with relief from looking into her friend's brown eyes. "Goodness, Ari! I stopped for like a minute or two, and you were gone!" She wrapped her arms around her friend, and after a second, Ariella returned the gesture.

"I'm sorry," Ariella said as she began to let go.

Daisy pulled herself away from the hug. "I thought you went back inside the school." She laughed hysterically, tears streaming through her ruined makeup. "I thought you'd gone back inside for Connor."

Ariella joined in the laughter, wrapping an arm over Daisy's shoulders. "I thought I told you. He texted me. He's perfectly fine!" She waited till her laughter slowed before asking, "But why Connor? That's so random."

Daisy's eyes found a tree off in the distance. "Oh, he has our project, so I thought you'd still be worrying about that." Now was not the time to say she'd thought her friend had gone back inside for a simple crush. She grabbed her phone only to see that it was bombarded by a flurry of texts from her mom. "My mom is giving us a ride. Text me your address."

Ariella sighed deeply and pulled out her now heavily cracked phone. "I'm disappointed in you, Dais. We've been best friends for half a decade, and you still haven't memorized my address."

Daisy rolled her eyes and tried to follow the instructions her mom had left her.

Brittanyb813: im here
Brittanyb813: where ru
Brittanyb813: ru here
Brittanyb813: nvr mind, come to the lot

Brittanyb813: the one with the big tee

Brittanyb813: *tree

Brittanyb813: and the bell

Brittanyb813: the front on i think

Brittanyb813: hurry plz jj hungry

"She types worse than you," Daisy said, shaking her head at the disfigured messages.

Ariella leaned onto Daisy's shoulder and winced. "Yeah. Does she not know about location sharing?"

"I tried," Daisy told her as they began their trek to the front lot. "But you know how parents are."

"Do I ever." Ariella took a look at Daisy's ripped-up backpack. "Lucky for me, my dad works in tech."

"So does mine," Daisy said dryly, and Ariella quickly tried to change the subject.

"Texted you my address," Ariella told her, and she made a big show of looking for the car. "It's black, right?"

Daisy sighed and nodded. "Yep, but looks more like a dirty gray. Needs a good wash."

Both girls scanned the lot, eyes glazing over the chaos that came with having your school bombed midday. Ariella pointed out the big tree that had been mentioned in the texts. "She's probably behind that big pickup truck," the brunette said, dragging her friend along. Daisy's green braids whooshed in the wind as they raced over to the car. She got there just fast enough to claim shotgun. Ariella hopped in next to JJ.

"Thank Raji you two are here," Brittany said from her spot in the driver's seat, starting the car. "I was just about ready to go down and grab you two myself."

Ariella chuckled politely, but Daisy rolled her eyes at the window. Ariella looked at JJ, who was playing a game on his tablet. "What were you two doing before you had to pick us up?"

"He was watching his show, and I was doing makeup," Brittany proclaimed, answering for him. "I heard that the bomb was planted by the Black Claws. Is that true?"

Daisy watched in the rearview mirror as Ariella shrugged before realizing that Brittany wasn't allowed to turn around in the car and look at her while driving. "That's what the principal says, but it's still an open investigation."

Daisy blew a puff of air out of her lips. "Some girl who was running like a maniac down the hill told me that she saw some guy set a vat of oil on fire. She seemed slightly delusional."

Brittany let out one of her *I-am-still-very-young-and-act-like-a-teenager* laughs, perfectly white teeth glinting in the light. It wasn't really that funny. Even JJ knew it. Daisy caught him raising an eyebrow in the rearview mirror. She chuckled and immediately regretted it because it started her mom on another round of laughing.

"Are you okay, Ms. Pierre-Harper?" Ariella asked. "I have water if you need some." Daisy was impressed that she remembered their full last name (nobody did) and that she didn't call her Mrs. Pierre-Harper instead. Brittany did not like to have any reminder of Daisy's dad in the least.

Brittany abruptly stopped her laugh. "Sea star, you're a dear." Daisy gagged inwardly from the nickname, feeling deeply for her friend. "But Daisy here is just so gosh darn funny. You should know by now to call me Brittany."

Ariella, always one for politeness, hesitated. "Are you sure? I'd hate to overstep."

Brittany waved a hand, and Daisy wished that she'd stop doing that and keep her hands on the wheel. It could be the reason all four of them got into an accident. Just because Brit—er…Mom couldn't keep her hands on the wheel.

"Flower?"

Daisy gave her mom a side eye. "Yes?"

"I asked you if I need to make a right at this next light."

"Why not ask Ariella?" Daisy asked, refusing to look away from the window. "It's her house!"

"That's no way to talk to your mother!" Brittany's face had a dusting of scarlet on it. "All I asked is where I'm supposed to turn!"

Daisy sighed and scrambled to grab her phone, pulling up the address on the maps app. "Um...no, don't turn right." The map began tilting to the left on her screen, and she groaned. "I mean, yeah. The map was acting up."

Brittany looked up at the light, which was turning red, and booked it. She pressed on the gas and slammed the car to the right despite the assortment of honks. "Well, that was close, wasn't it?"

Poor Ariella. Her face was pale, as if she were about to puke. JJ wasn't even phased, still refusing to look up from his tablet. "Make a left in about a thousand feet," Daisy told her as they began going through the neighborhood. "Not this upcoming left but the left after that." Brittany barely slowed down her driving, going from maniac speed to main road speed. "Mom! We're still in a neighborhood. Slow down!"

Brittany shot her daughter a look. "And whose fault is it for not showing up on time? I can't be late for my appointment."

"Oh please," Daisy said, rolling her eyes instead of continuing the argument.

"Um." Mother and daughter turned to look at Ariella fingering a curl. "My house is the green one on the left. If you just pull into the driveway, that'd be great!"

Brittany put on her *I'm-so-amazing-and-I'm-an-amazing-mom* smile. "Of course, sea star. You can get out right now."

Ariella practically sprinted out of the car, desperate to get away from the spat that was bound to happen. "Bye! Thanks for the ride, Brittany!" And there she went, racing up the steps and through the door.

Brittany's *I'm-so-amazing-and-I'm-an-amazing-mom* smile stayed firmly in place until they pulled away and were safely down the road. "Honestly, I can't believe you'd say something like that!"

"Like what?" Daisy shot back, equally mad at her mom. "The fact that you said it's my fault for being late when I was the one who just got attacked at school?"

Brittany scoffed as she hammered the car into a sharp right. "The fact that you'd try and instigate an argument while we have a guest in the car. Do you understand the kind of pressure that puts me under?"

Daisy snorted, snot spilling out of her nose.

"Wipe that up. Not with your sleeve. Thank you," Brittany said.

Daisy rolled her eyes. It wasn't like she was a germaphobe at home. Her bathroom sink was littered with makeup supplies. "I'm sorry for embarrassing you in front of my friend," she told her mom, malice tinting her voice. "Can't imagine how mortifying that must have been."

Another jerk of the steering wheel, and they were at the side of their house. "In case you were wondering," Brittany told her, eyes glittering with rage, "I did leave something in the fridge this time."

Daisy smiled sweetly. "Glad you're finally learning how to be a mom." She got out of the car and slammed her car door as loudly as possible (which wasn't very loud because the door was broken) and stalked off to the house's entrance. JJ followed behind her, still on his tablet.

Brittany probably yelled something back, something that probably would've hurt her daughter to her core, but Daisy sped away, so it just sounded like a big bundle of loudness. She watched the car drive off in a big huff of smoke, and once she was sure it was gone, she opened the door, which Brittany had forgotten to lock. "Let's go inside, JJ."

JJ finally looked up from his screen as he made his way up the steps. "I'm hungwy," he announced to Daisy as they walked inside.

Daisy locked the door and made her way to the kitchen. "Mom said she left stuff in the fridge. We'll see if it's edible this time."

"But I don't wanna eat wice," he told her worriedly.

"Did she seriously just leave that little bowl of rice for dinner?" Daisy asked, annoyed.

"Yeah." JJ was back on his tablet, making his way over to the couch. "Owange chicken too."

Well, at least she left protein this time. That was an improvement. Daisy opened the fridge to see the smallest takeout box of orange chicken and rice, barely enough for one person.

"Guess I'm making dinner again."

A RIELLA LOOKED AROUND FROM HER spot on the dirt, trying to tune out the principal's attempt to entertain teenagers before they began their big announcement. Camera crews surrounded the stage, getting the equipment ready for the big finale. Unfortunately, the principal had assumed that since their cameras were angled towards him (even though they weren't on yet), he was on national television.

The principal himself was standing on a makeshift stage. It didn't look makeshift however, wood planks polished to perfection. It hadn't been here the day before. In fact, after the smoke and debris were cleared away, Areilla realized that the whole third floor of the school had collapsed (and part of the second). It looked as though a plane had flown through it, taking care to destroy as much of the building as possible.

All of the students who'd made it out alive from the attack were instructed to meet by the school's main entrance and to stand on what used to be a bright green lawn. That one little five letter word spelled a-l-i-v-e. Alive. There were some students who weren't alive. Some whose bodies were never going to take another step or breathe another breath. It was terrifying to think that that may have been her, that it could have been Daisy.

"...We will always stand strong despite the attempts to break our will. We are the Raghunathan Collective Society," the principal said, his voice breaking through her depressing line of thought. "We are..."

Ariella tuned him out again, checking her phone for the time. Five minutes until the big announcement. Five minutes until she needed to be listening. The announcement was to come straight from Queen Rajikumari herself, explaining how they'd get through this tough time together. The news about the bombing had been broadcast around the nation last night, sending a shockwave of grief.

Someone placed a hand on her shoulder, making her turn around. "Did it start yet?" Daisy whispered. "I had to get JJ ready for school since Brittany had work."

Ariella shook her head and checked her phone. "Three minutes left." She made a vague gesture in the direction of the makeshift stage. "You missed most of his attempts to bond us together. Anyone with eyes could tell someone had written the speech for him this morning."

Daisy chuckled and sat on the dirt next to Ariella. "Is the queen actually coming to talk, or is it a hologram like usual?"

Ariella checked her phone once again, internally sighing at all the cracks. "We'll see in two minutes." The digital clock ticked forward, and she corrected herself. "Actually, one minute."

Since the stage had been hurriedly put up the night before and the fact that it was outdoors, Ariella was able to see the vice principal in the "backstage" area. The vice principal tapped at her watch and gestured for the principal to come off the stage. The stagehands nodded and walked towards him. "And remember, kids," he said as he was getting directed off like a toddler. "RCS forever!"

It was silent on the stage for a little while as thousands of eyes watched for someone to come. People looked up from their phones, the quiet drawing their eyes to the spotlight in the middle of the stage. The stagehands pulled together makeshift curtains. They waited, eyes on the ground before slowly pulling the curtains apart again.

That's when the crowd saw her, golden crown gleaming and high heels clicking. Her black dress flowed like water to her ankles, allowing a glimpse of her golden heels. Her RCS pin looked even more magnificent than in the hologram, the triangle barely able to contain the paw print. Her hair was in the tightest bun known to man, not a single strand of ebony out of place. Her face was youthful, but her expression held the lines that one could only get from decades of strife. Her eyes were the color of ravens, as dark as the pencil that shaped her brows. The glittering gold of the negative space liner and the spider-like length of her lashes made her look celestial. She was gorgeous and dangerous, dainty and noble, feminine and formidable. When she reached the microphone, her voice was a commanding presence. "All rise for your queen." Anyone sitting on the grass rose. "All rise for the Raghunathan Collective Society, the RCS." Everyone had their eyes locked on her. "I hereby pledge to forever and always," she began, head tilted slightly towards the students, waiting for their answer.

"I hereby pledge to forever and always," they all chanted back, voices joining together in harmony.

"Devote all my support," she went on, the words booming off the microphone.

"Devote all my support."

"To our mighty leader." A small smile wove its way through her features, messing with her picture-perfect jawline and making her feel human.

"To our mighty leader." They were all louder than ever now, waiting for the crescendo.

"Queen Rajikumari Raghunathan the Third." Her eyes had a glint of pride in them as she looked over them like a mother hen looked over her chicks.

"Queen Rajikumari Raghunathan the Third," her chicks chirped back.

The queen's lips curved further upwards, stretching her skin from side to side and wrinkling her makeup slightly. "Meus es in aeternum." Her left hand joined her right to make a triangle over the symbolic pin on her heart. "RCS forever."

Everyone joined her, all making the triangle over their hearts. "RCS forever."

A beat of quiet settled over them, triangles cracking in half and becoming hands again. Once the last triangle faded away, Queen Rajikumari let her own hands fall to her sides. Her smile slowly faded into something of a grimace before she began talking. "As all of you know, I am Queen Rajikumari Raghunathan the Third." A strategic silence followed, giving everyone the chance to watch the grimace tip into an upside-down grin. "I wish I could have met you all under better circumstances." A murmur of agreement was heard throughout the crowd. "But as fate would have it…" She used the word fate like all blame and misgivings could be tossed aside through the careful use of it. "The atrocious acts made against us by that group of conspirators, known to us as the Black Claws, are the very thing that has brought us together as one." A well-placed pause occurred. "It is with great sorrow that I tell you their act took the lives of twenty-one proud citizens, both adolescents and adults alike. But their spirit will live on with us forever. They tried to shatter us, but we have something they don't." Her jawline was fully in place again, looking like a goddess cut from diamond. "Unity. Their attacks may have caught us off guard, but when we fight as one, we are unstoppable."

Everyone knew what was coming next, chanting with her as she finished, "WE ARE RCS FOREVER."

That proud smile came again, twitching at the corners of her mouth. "I see that this school has taught you well. I pray that you all will be ready for what lies ahead." Her hand made a wide gesture, trying to encompass her entire nation in a simple sweep of her arm. "You all remember our upbringing. How we were on the brink of losing to the BPR when our scientists made our biggest breakthrough." Her eyes had a faraway gleam to them, as if transported back into those fateful days, though she hadn't been alive at that time. "They were the reason we were able to create the antimatter bomb, and for that, we are in their eternal debt."

"My great-grandfather, Rahemun Raghunathan the First, fought in the war." As she stood, she crossed her right leg over her left, golden high heels hitting the light as if the sun were her personal servant. "He led his soldiers into battle. He was with the team that dropped the Bomb." She looked over the crowd, and everyone felt as though she were looking at them in particular. "He wanted the youth of today to continue protecting the nation. That's why my great-grandfather created the Juvenile Security Program, the JSP." The queen pressed both hands to her chest before continuing, "You all have heard about the program. You all know someone who's gone through the tests."

Her tongue slithered around the next words, venom felt with each and every word. "But the Black Claws didn't like that. They don't like that I want to find potential in each and every one of you." Her eyes went dark, like the sun had set for her and her alone. "They think kids are just kids. They think I'm unethical." She had to rein herself in. She had to be the queen everyone else always saw when they looked at her.

Impassible. Immaculate. Infallible.

"But that's why they bombed the school, to show how angry—" Queen Rajikumari clapped her hands together like a bolt of lightning, her high heels shifting to catch the light again. "They are about these mandatory tests, how much fury they had for my great-grandfather's program." She let the top lip quirk to the side, careful to keep her dimples at bay. A queen made of stone did not have dimples when she smirked. "They say they wanted to protect today's youth, so that's why they bombed a high school."

She let that sink in. People didn't like it when you pointed out the obvious to them. They liked to be the ones to piece together the puzzle. They liked to feel smart. So she let them. She knew who was really in control anyway. "They want me to be scared. They want you to be terrified." She cocked her head at them, giving each person a knowing look. "But none of us will back down, will we?"

They all stared back at her, and she repeated her question, even though they all knew it had one answer. "None of us will give in, will we?" She could see the children shook their heads in the crowd. Good. Her tone became more sympathetic as she touched on another topic. "Our comrades who were snatched into the sky too soon, they wouldn't want us to give in, would they? Would they want us to listen to the monsters that took them?"

The queen eyed the sky, head tilted just so to make it seem as if she were looking directly at the sun, directly at the people who had tragically perished. "I think we need to reinstate the pride we once had for this country. I think we've gotten complacent. Don't you?" She was looking at them again, piercing them with her ebony eyes. "That's why I think we need to start the tests this week to show the Black Claws that we are not weak."

People whispered to each other while looking nervously at her stone-cold face. "Let me explain to you what is going to happen, what we are doing to prove our loyalty to the RCS." A thoughtful look crossed her face as she went on, like she was formulating the plan here and now. "Everyone above the age of fifteen is required to take the tests, and the tests themselves are broken up into three stages." She flicked her eyes over to the principal and jutted her head at him. "The first stage is simple. Things that you should know from school and life." The queen looked out at the crowd before locking eyes with a girl and winking, golden eyelid gleaming. "Fitness tests, literary tests, simple things like that." She walked around the stage, fingers curving around the microphone like a hawk catching its prey. "I think that should be easy for everyone."

Nervous chatter came from behind the stage, the faculty now wondering how this would affect them, wondering if they might be punished for students not doing well. She turned her head towards them, serving them a dangerous smile with an extra side of pearly white teeth. "Anything important you all need to tell me? I'd really like to get on with the speech." Her mouth was off the mic. Only they could hear her.

Timid squirrelly eyes looked back at her, terrified of her wrath. They all shook their heads, mouths zipped shut. The queen nodded curtly and gave them one last grin, canines gleaning. "Glad we're all on the same page." She turned back to her loyal students, all of them gazing upon her. "There will be a multitude of tests on that first day. The top hundred or so will move on."

Their faces turned ghostly, scared by what she wasn't saying about those who didn't make it. To reassure them, she moved her hand dismissively, letting out a loud laugh. "Nothing bad will happen if you aren't at the top. Don't look so frightened." They laughed with her, first forced and then for real. Good. "The next test will be at the JSP headquarters. It'll be harder, more challenging. Only a few will make it to the last level." She narrowed her eyes, pupils scanning for potential winners. A few stood out, but it was nearly impossible to tell what lay on the inside when you looked at someone's outsides. "Those last few will be tested for the field, for the missions you might get sent on."

The queen used her free hand to make another dismissive sweep across the room. "Before each test, you will get a thorough explanation of the rules. You will get time to meditate on how to pass." She looked up at the sky and chuckled. "Do I seem like the person to throw you in blind?" Nobody answered, and she knew what they all were thinking. She was good like that. "I promise that nobody will get hurt. We do not kill our own kind. We make them stronger." With that solemn oath, she gave them some more tidbits about what to expect. Just enough to calm panic but not enough to stop nerves. "For those who pass all three stages, you will be sent on missions. You are always allowed to say no." She gave a lighthearted shrug, shoulders moving just enough to make her dress twirl around her. "But you're giving up making a difference. You're giving up the opportunity to make our nation a greater place. Just keep that in mind if you're blessed with the possibility of making that choice."

It was time to change tactics. Her face became stricken with lines of grief. Not too many though. She still was their leader after all. "We obviously won't be using the school for the first round of tests. We don't want to be victims of another heinous attack by the Black Claws, do we?" The question was supposed to be rhetorical, but people nodded in agreement. "I have faith that your principal will find a new and safe place for you all to complete these tests. The remainder of today will be spent mourning the loss that befell us." She gave a wave with her golden nails and made her way off the stage, crown poised and dress flowing just the right amount.

She looked perfect. She was perfect. She is *perfect*.

"I wish you all the best of luck. Just remember—"

"WE ARE RCS FOREVER!" they all shouted for her, making her grin ear to ear, dimples be damned.

She walked off the stage, disappearing from view and away to wherever she was needed next. They were all quiet, waiting for the click of her high heels to fade away. When the sound finally did, their principal lugged himself onto the stage. "You heard the queen. The rest of this day will be empty for grieving. We will contact your parents about the details for the tests tomorrow." He raised his fist in the air. "RCS forever!"

Nobody chanted along with him, all sharing awkward looks from his attempt to end with a bang. Realizing that he did not have nearly as much stage presence as Queen Rajikumari, he fled from the stage, cheeks flushed with embarrassment.

Slowly but surely, the crowds began to disperse, leaving just a few students standing by themselves. Without the queen standing there and guiding them, a sense of despair settled over the remaining people. They would never see their dead classmates ever again. Ariella wished she could say that she was crying, or at least had some sign that she was visibly in despair. But she didn't really feel anything, mainly because nothing had happened to her or people she knew. If anything, she felt relief.

Ariella was among those students still standing around because in a shocking turn of events, Brittany was there before her mom, and Daisy had actually been among the first to leave. Daisy had offered a ride to her, but Ariella had been under the impression that her ride would be arriving soon. Brittany's early arrival probably had to do with the fact that she was extremely keen on catching a glimpse of Queen Rajikumari herself. Ariella chuckled at the thought of Brittany getting a chance to fangirl over the queen. That'd be something she'd pay to watch. But it wasn't nice to think about Daisy's mom like that because…Ariella thought about all the times Daisy had made her stay up late and rant about Brittany forgetting to pick her up, or Brittany not being back home until the early hours of the morning, and she felt a little better about thinking that. Her phone buzzed, and she looked at it, hoping that it would tell her that her ride was here.

eli;32: i just left

Her parents were at work right now, so that left her brother. She hated his car. It was an oldie he'd tried to fix himself, and it always smelled like gasoline, but he insisted that's how "real" cars were supposed to smell. One of these days, she'd pass out from the smell. Just fall right there in her seat with her neck tilted to one of those grotesque angles.

Ariella leaned back onto the grass, giving herself over to the bugs and gross things that lived there. Her mind wandered to the speech she'd just witnessed. It was thrilling to see Queen Rajikumari in person, even if she was just in the crowd. The way she was able to rally so many different people together in just a short five-minute span was incredible. Her presence was...Ariella thought for a second, trying to think about the best word to encompass her. Alluring. Queen Rajikumari was alluring. It was the way she could keep you hanging onto every word with just a sentence. It was the way she made you feel so strongly about something you barely knew anything about. It was the way she knew you.

Ariella felt a sting and realized that there was something on her leg. A spider to be exact. She brushed it off and decided that was enough grass for one day. She began to get antsy, walking back and forth in the stage area while she waited.

That's when the rain began. Skipping the step where it was supposed to flow in little drizzles, the rain poured onto her head. Good Raji, she should've just accepted the ride from Brittany. The previous day floated into her head, reminding her of her conversation with Daisy when she was jumping in all of the puddles. Ariella looked at her broken screen as she made a run for the underside of the stage. No messages popped up, and she groaned, squeezing herself into the only semi-dry place. She curled herself into a ball, feeling all the heavy droplets of water seeping in through the cracks. When she finally reached a small level of comfort, her phone buzzed.

eli;32: here
eli;32: hello
eli;32: im oniy stayin for like 5 min
eli;32: only

Ariella texted back a quick acknowledgement and crawled out to the exit, trying to break out into a run. She fell. Bad. Her face got covered in mud. And her shirt and skirt and pretty much everything. She slowly pulled herself up and began to trudge up the hill, scared she might go tumbling down. When Ariella finally reached the car, which was parked right by the main entrance of the school, she looked like a mud monster.

"Mind telling me what the—" He caught himself and tried again. "What happened to you?" Eli asked, wincing as his seat got covered with her mud. "The monster finally got you?"

"You're not even funny," she told him, refusing to say anything more.

As he started the engine up again, she began to shiver. "Is the air conditioner on or something? It's cold as crap right now."

"I think it's just the mud," he told her. "Looks pretty fresh to me."

She tried to say something snarky back, but a fresh wave of gasoline hit her in the face as the car started up. What a way to end her day. Except for the fact that it was barely noon.

VII

CARMEN LOOKED UP AT THE CLOCK inside their makeshift classroom. Spoiler alert: It was inside the fifteenth floor of an office building. Twenty-seven seconds had passed since she last checked it. She scanned the room again. Everyone was hard at work, writing tools scratching the tests in front of them. To Carmen, it was a stupid test. She wasn't even sure how it'd help the RCS decide who was moving on to the next phase of tests. She looked up at the clock again. A full forty-three seconds had gone by this time. Maybe she should've paid more attention to the test instructors yesterday. But all she could remember was that they had four tests in one day. Who seriously spent a full school day explaining rules to teenagers? Her eyes wandered to the first question laid out on the page.

1. Which would you rather have: money or power?

It was a stupid question, at least in Carmen's opinion. How could you have money without power? Or did they mean power like being able to shoot fire out of your hands? And to keep that money, you needed some kind of power, right? Also, how many words did you need exactly for it to be considered a good answer? She was pretty sure the person on her left had at least written a full essay.

"Ten minutes left!" the person at the front of the room announced.

Carmen wasn't even sure what the test administrators were doing here since it seemed impossible to cheat on questions like this. Good Raji, she really only had ten minutes left for what? Seven questions? She looked at the question again and scrawled down her one-word answer. Wait, did she need more than one word? Sighing, she rolled her eyes and erased her one-word answer and wrote three words in its stead. Time for question number two.

2. Expand on the last question and explain *why* that was your answer.

Okay, so that wasn't even a question. Carmen looked up at the clock again. About a minute and thirty-eight seconds had passed since she last checked. She wrote another one-sentence answer and let her eyes roam around the room. Everyone was reading over their answers. That one person on her left had a smug grin as they turned their fully completed test over to read over their answers. Well, fuck them. This wasn't graded anyway. She went to the next question.

3. For a good nation to prosper, do you need money or power?

What was with the words "money" and "power?" Carmen looked longingly towards the front of the room, locking eyes with her pink-cased phone in the caddy. It sucked that they all had to turn their phones in, but test procedures were test procedures. She looked back at her answer for question one and copied that down. There! She could be smart if she wanted to.

4. Expand on the last question and explain *why* that was your answer.

Again, this wasn't a question. Yet for some reason, it demanded an answer. She looked back at her answer for number two before copying that down. Sure, some might call her lazy, but she called it being resourceful. Her eyes wandered to the clock again and gasped. Two minutes and fifty-four seconds had passed between now and the last time she'd laid eyes on it. No matter how stupid the tests were, she wasn't about to suffer consequences for leaving it blank.

"Shit!"

"No swearing!" the test administrator yelled from the front.

Guess she said that aloud. She gave them the evil eye before moving on to question five.

5. Which one would you pick: fame or influence?

Hey, they changed it up at last. She thought about the question for a second. Weren't they the same thing? At least in her mind, they were pretty damn similar. She looked at the clock. Thirty-three seconds. She watched the seconds hand tick along steadily before writing down her answer.

"Five minutes!"

Carmen swore they were looking dead at her when they called out.

6. Expand on the last question and explain *why* that was your answer.

Well, it was simple in her head, but it was hard to figure out the best way to place the words down on paper. She scrunched up her nose and used the pointy tip of her pencil to scratch the place where her scalp met her forehead. Whether they said it was graded or not, Carmen was pretty sure they wanted an answer. So she gave them one. Was it good? That was for them to decide. There, done. But she remembered with a sneer what the know-it-all to her left had been doing. She turned her paper to the back.

7. Which would be better for a kingdom: fame or influence?

Carmen copied down her previous answer before scanning over the next question. She could speed through this if she tried. Her ears picked up the sound of chairs rattling and footsteps heading to the door. She was definitely going to be the last one. She almost cursed loudly when she realized that there was yet another question to answer.

8. Using creative language, explain *why* you chose your answer to the last question.

Who in Rajikumari's name did they think she was? The queen's firstborn daughter? Why would she have "creative language" in her? She couldn't write poems. Carmen looked up, and the clock told her she'd better try.

"Fifteen seconds!" the test administrator called out when she finished.

She got up to turn it in, pushing through the empty desks to get to the front. Test Administrator gave her a raised eyebrow. "Finished in the nick of time?"

"Better to be fashionably late than never show up at all," she shot back, smiling. She snatched her phone out of the caddy. They probably said something back, or maybe they didn't. Carmen slammed the door too hard to hear the test administrator. On the bright side, she'd never have to see them again! She'd fail the test (probably) and have a four-day weekend while everyone else did whatever happened to those who passed. A terrible thought struck as she made her way to the elevator. What if Queen Raji was lying? Would she really just let people off for not trying? She rolled her eyes at the notion. Maybe she under-exaggerated how little consequence there was for failing, but Queen Raji would never tell a bold-faced lie. All great leaders had to embellish things sometimes.

Carmen looked back at the closing doors of the elevator and swore, doing a quick walk in her brown leather platform heels. Thinking quickly, she flung the one thing on her back through the small gap between the door. Her backpack landed on the floor with a thud, and the elevator doors opened. The crowd in the elevator glared at her, but she couldn't care less. "Thanks for waiting," she told them, crouching down to pick up her backpack.

Someone stepped on her hand when it touched the floor. Carmen looked up from her crouched position to meet the eyes of a middle-aged man. She supposed some of the higher-ranking office workers still had to come to work while they were testing. "Sorry, missy." His eyes told her he was not at all sorry. "Didn't see you there."

She bit her tongue and ignored him, pressing twenty-six on the elevator. The doors opened at floor eighteen, letting off two kids and a woman with really tall boots (Carmen recognized the pair of boots from her birthday wishlist). A mom with a baby wrapped to her chest and a two-year-old boy hopped on, and she pressed for the twenty-third floor. Carmen was confused about the fact that there were children on the elevator until she remembered the map pointing out that there was a daycare for parents who needed childcare while working. They had been explicitly told not to go on that floor.

"Careful," Middle-Aged Man told the two-year-old. "Don't want you messing up my new shoes."

Yeah, better not mess up the shoes you used to maliciously step on a teenage girl's hand with. But Carmen only kept a calm grimace on her face as the mom chuckled nervously. "Sorry, tight space here."

Middle-Aged Man offered her a grunt in return. "I'm warning ya."

Queen of the RCS, they all got it. His shoes were supposed to be their sole priority on this packed elevator. The elevator stopped on floor twenty-two, and a nicer-looking middle-aged man squeezed his way to the front, careful to avoid the brand new shoes. He was probably a people pleaser, Carmen snorted to herself at the thought.

A student with a large backpack walked on, pressing the button for floor eighteen. Their backpack brushed against the two-year-old's face, making his heel come down on Middle-Aged Man's left shoe. "You brat! I warned you not to step on my—"

The elevator opened at twenty-three, and the mom fled out, her baby bouncing up and down. Well, look at that. His poor dress shoes had a boo-boo. Maybe if he didn't want anything to get messed up, he should've taken the stairs. Carmen looked at his salt and pepper beard and guessed that he was the type of guy to complain about kids playing in a park.

"Little kids are so unpredictable, am I right?" he said, the fakest chuckle escaping from his lips. Nobody offered him a chuckle back. "I did warn him," Middle-Aged Man tried again. "It wasn't like I yelled out of nowhere."

Carmen just about had it with him. She turned toward him with a grin. "Teenagers too," she told him, leg twitching in anticipation. "They can be terribly unpredictable."

He looked at her, slightly confused. That's when her chunky heel came crashing down on his right foot, making him howl in pain. The elevator doors opened, and Carmen bolted into the hallway. "You bitch!" he yelled after her.

A quick look behind her shoulder let her know that he had begun to run after her. Great. She loved running in her sky-high platforms.

"I had these shoes specially made from Queen Raji's palace!"

"I sincerely doubt that," Carmen yelled back, turning a sharp right. "You look like an average office worker to me!" Up ahead was a women's restroom. She just needed to get inside and lock it. Good Raji, what possessed her to do that anyway? The kid had already "ruined" his shoes. "When I catch up to you, you'll regret having ever touched my shoes," Carmen heard from behind her. How did she always find herself in situations like this? Here she was, in the middle of floor... twenty-five? Twenty-six? And she was being chased in a makeshift school by an old man who was probably counting down the days till he retired. She sneaked a look behind her again. Good Raji, he was gaining on her.

"Sorry for interrupting your tests," the loudspeaker blared. Fuck, she was late for her test, wasn't she? That bell must have rung when she was in the elevator. "But would a Carmen Orlovski report to the head office on floor twenty-five?"

She was officially dead. "Here lies Carmen Orlovski," she muttered to herself as she made a left towards what she hoped would be the head office. "She died from stepping on a middle-aged man's shoe. Poor thing."

A door about twenty-five feet ahead opened. That better be the main office door, Carmen thought. She could hear the ragged breathing of someone gaining on her, and that's when she knew she had to actually run instead of doing a fast waddle. Sure, she could pull off a badass strut in heels. But running? She looked like the ugly duckling trying to fly. Utterly pitiful.

By some miracle, she reached the door first. A person pulled open the door for her, and she went in. She didn't even have time to give him the finger before slamming the door shut, hearing the satisfying sound of an automatic lock. Once she was sure he'd stalked off towards his next victim, she slid herself down to the bottom of the door. Air went into her lungs and came out of her mouth as she calmed herself down. A hand came into her peripheral vision, and Carmen grabbed it. Her feet were tingling like they were on fire as they helped pull her up, any adrenaline gone from her system.

"Well, that was eventful, wasn't it?" the person attached to the hand asked her. She began shaking her hand rapidly as if she were on fire herself. "I'm Kai Kinkade, the lead analyzer of that paper test you just took."

Carmen gulped nervously, pasting on a cocky smile. "If you've analyzed the results already, I'd say you're pretty good at your job." Flattery always helped soften a blow when you were in a pickle. Not too much though. People didn't like being lied to.

A small smile wove its way across her lips. She let go of Carmen's hand and ran hers over her perfectly gelled down red hair, bun so tight it looked like it might burst. "I have a team of highly trained advisors as well. They just send me the tests that are unique."

Carmen was nervous. Hers was probably unique in all the wrong ways. "What about mine caught their eye?" she tried, eyes crinkling in confusion. "I'm sure there were much more insightful tests." Modesty was also a trait that people in power just gobbled up from children.

Kai walked off, making Carmen follow her through the desks to an office enclosed in glass. She opened the door for Carmen before following her into the room. "Please, sit wherever you'd like," Kai told her guest, taking the chair behind the desk.

Carmen looked at her options: a stiff-looking easy chair in the corner and a swivel chair in front of Kai. She took the swivel chair, subtly angling it towards the door. You could never be too careful with certain people.

"You must be wondering why you're here," Kai said, a genuine smile covering her face. "Aren't you?"

No, not exactly. She'd literally just told Carmen that she only looked at unique tests. But Carmen didn't say that. "Well, I am a little confused," she fingered her purple and blue bracelet. "Didn't you say it had something to do with being... unique?" She hoped her eyes had that confusion sparkling in them too. Eyes could sell anything.

Kai nodded enthusiastically. "Exactly. The reason I called you in here is because I wanted to go over a couple of your test answers in more detail."

Well, that didn't sound too terrible, did it? But then again, the Kai lady could probably be smiling in the middle of a forest fire. "Could you explain what caught your eye?" Carmen's tongue licked her molars, eyes tilted towards the window in the corner. "I'm not a great test taker." Her hand rubbed the back of her neck, making her eyes meet the plastic table.

Kai scoffed at her words and pulled out a piece of paper. Carmen assumed that someone must have brought her the test before she'd called Carmen up here. "Your answer to question number one. Explain more of what you meant by that."

"And what exactly did question one say?" Carmen asked, not liking how she couldn't predict where this was going.

Kai cleared her throat and read it aloud: "Which would you rather have: power or money?"

"And what did I say?" Carmen remembered exactly what she'd said now, but she wanted to hear Kai say it herself.

"You said I'd choose both, but the question only lets you pick one answer." Kai seemed intrigued.

Not the reaction Carmen had expected at all. To keep up the innocent act or drop it? Kai seemed like she loved a little lamb, so why not give her what she liked? "Well, I was worried it would be seemingly too bold." She almost threw up in her mouth from those words and toned down the self-deprecation. "But I just don't see why you can't have one without the other, especially in our society today."

"You're saying that you need both. You can't live without one unless you have the other?" Kai's voice seemed less chipper and more judgmental.

"I'm saying that realistically, a person can't have a shi—" Kai's little lamb wouldn't swear. She quickly self-corrected herself and said, "Shipload of money without a lot of power and vice versa."

"But we weren't asking you to be realistic. We were asking which one you would choose," Kai told her, eyes flashing with an excited kind of fire.

"But you can't choose." Carmen was losing her grip on the mask now. "Why would I prefer one over the other when they're both intertwined? You can't have one without the other."

"But they aren't the same thing." Kai's voice made Carmen want to strangle her. It was highly infuriating. "Money is used to spend things, and power gives you control over people. You can have one without the other."

"But what if you want to be more than just a shitty office worker?" Crap, she wasn't supposed to be swearing. She was supposed to be the smart little lamb who could charm herself out of anything. She was supposed to be untouchable. "You need some kind of power to help get you to the top, either your own or someone else's. How else did you get your job?" Kai tried to talk, but Carmen clapped her hands together, refusing to be steamrolled. "You knew someone. You had leverage. You had power." Her eyes went back towards the window, eyes watching a little gray bird fly past. "That power. It got you money." She shot her eyes back to Kai, challenging her to refute her.

"But that's not what we were asking for," Kai insisted, and Carmen knew that the redhead wasn't as chipper as she made herself out to be. "We were asking which one you'd choose, not about how I got my job or if you wanted to be a shitty office worker." She did quotation marks with her fingers for the last bit.

"Then tell me, Ms. Kai Kitashi." She was pretty sure that was the wrong last name, but she couldn't care less. "Which one would you choose? Which one would you get further with?"

"It's Kai Kinkade," she corrected. "And that's not the question." She looked back at that stupid piece of paper. "Question one: Explain in your own—"

"Just stop," Carmen interrupted, sick of her repeating the same thing over again. "If you had absolutely no money and all the power, you'd lose influence. People would rather look up to a golden statue than a pile of horse poop." She was livid, Kai having pushed all her buttons at once. "If you had all the money but no power, the people in power wouldn't let you keep it. Since they have influence, your money wouldn't help you." She glared daggers at the woman in front of her. "I'm sure there's a better way to say it, but that's my opinion."

A slow, smug smile found its way to Kai's face. "Looks like my advisors were right. We've got a firecracker here." She clicked her tongue and chuckled. "If it weren't for them, I would've fallen for this act, hook, line, and sinker."

Ouch. She'd definitely underestimated Kai. She did a slow, sarcastic golf clap. "Congrats! You are person number 436 to get Carmen to explode." She curled her upper lip in disgust. "Does that make you happy?"

"Oh, feisty too." Kai rolled her eyes playfully. "I'm sure you'd like to know the full reason I called you in here."

Carmen raised an eyebrow, using her hand to gesture for her to continue. "I'm waiting."

"Sure, lots of people put down that answer for question one, but when they get called in, they can't explain why." Kai tapped at her head with her index finger. "That's why I prodded you. I wanted to see if you'd stick with your answer despite me telling you otherwise."

"But you said you almost fell for my pretty princess act."

Kai let out a real laugh, left eye watering slightly when she finished. "Yes, I did, but that's why I pressed. Most people have buttons. You just have to know where to look for them. You do need to work on your temper. That won't help keep you in power."

Carmen pushed her chair back and placed her shoes on the desk, willing Kai to have a reaction. "Well, it was worth a try, I suppose." She pulled out her phone. "I think I have an athletic test I'm late for, so if there's any more curveballs you need to throw at me, make it quick." She grinned widely at Kai, taking pride in the way she flinched slightly from Carmen's quick change in demeanor.

"Oh, I guess I wasn't clear enough." Kai handed Carmen a badge. "You made it to the next round. Pack a bag of essentials for a week and come here at 7 a.m. for the bus. Congratulations on being the thirty-fifth person to pass." She glanced at Carmen's platforms. "Nice shoes."

Carmen scoffed and pulled them off the desk. "Thanks for passing me. Have a good rest of your day."

"You too!" Kai shouted back, the vigor making Carmen want to strangle her for the second time that day. "Loved your attempt at the haiku on question eight. Hilariously sad."

Carmen unlocked the handle and swung the door open. Hard. The handle slammed into the wall behind it and stayed there, leaving the door open. She winced. "Hope you have enough money *or* power to figure this out. I sure don't want to see you again."

And she strutted out the door, blowing the steaming red head a kiss for good measure. "Ta-ta!"

VIII

SHE WAS LUCKY TO EVEN BE HERE, Fernanda reminded herself after attempting to count to ten backwards. Lucky to have made it to the next round of the testing. And yes, when she had first arrived at the RCS Juvenile Security Program headquarters, she felt thoroughly lucky. Lucky to look up at the floor-to-ceiling length glass that covered all the levels of the skyscraper, which also housed the students. Lucky to get her very own key card for her very own room. Lucky to have a room on the highest floor, to have the thrill of looking down at the earth from her perch before bed.

But that was before she met her roommate. Her randomly assigned roommate.

"I think we gotta go now," the magenta-haired girl said to Fernanda. "We have ten minutes till orientation."

Fernanda looked up from her phone and faced her roommate. "And? The orientation is like a three-minute walk away."

"But lots of kids will be walking late," her roommate argued. "I'd really prefer to be early."

Fernanda was sure the girl would've been in the orientation room if it weren't for the fact that she was, without a doubt, the kind of person who wanted to be best friends with her roommate. Unfortunately, she was about to have another thing coming. "Well, I don't care about being early. They didn't say you'll be punished if you're late," Fernanda told her listlessly, feet dangling off the edge of her bed.

"Did you even glance at the manual?" Good Raji, her roommate's voice could be so high-pitched. When Fernanda shook her head, she shrieked again. "You're even worse at reading than me!" She grabbed the manual and pointed at the cover. "Can you read that? It says in all caps, *IF YOU'RE LATE, THEN YOU WILL BE SENT HOME!*"

Fernanda leapt off the edge of the top bunk, landing in a mangled squat. "And you never thought to tell me that?" She raced to put her sneakers on, ignoring her throbbing ankles.

The pink-haired girl was already holding the door open, letting Fernanda walk into the hallway first. "Calm down, High Pon…Fernanda. We'll get there fast."

Fernanda gave her an odd look, running her nails along the hallway wall as she walked. "What were you about to call me? The high something?"

Her roommate scratched nervously at her scalp. "It's nothing. Just got…got stuff mixed around in my head. Confusing, ya know?"

"But you literally just called me high?" Fernanda gasped and gave her a sideways glance, scooting away. "Do you think I do drugs? I swear if that's what Jack told you—"

"No, I don't think you're high!" She seemed exasperated now, dodging a girl who slammed their room door open. "Me and my friends heard from Lizzie—"

"And what'd she say?" Fernanda interrupted, eyes glinting with malice. "That blonde bitch thinks she's the ruler of our school or something. I'm telling you, her nails are just a bad knockoff of the queen's."

"Lizzie is not a blonde bitch! She's just misunderstood sometimes," the pink-haired girl shot back, hands doing angry gestures.

"Fine then," Fernanda huffed, refusing to look her in the eye. She stopped letting her nails scratch the walls as she walked, running them over her arms instead. "I guess she swindled you over to her side like she did to Jack, am I right?"

"Actually, I've been friends with Lizzie since grade school, so she didn't swindle me anywhere!"

The girl's face almost turned as purple as a rotten grape. It did not suit her very well.

"No wonder you're so brain dead," Fernanda called back, opening the door that had bright gold letters spelling out ORIENTATION MEETING ROOM. "You've been stuck doing Lizzie's bidding for who knows how long. It's sickening."

"I DON'T DO LIZZIE'S BIDDING!" Her words echoed around the auditorium, drawing eyes to the odd pair.

Fine, if her roommate could yell, then she could scream. "SAYS THE PERSON WHO MAKES HER LIVING BY TALKING SHIT FOR HER!"

Her roommate said nothing back, but she made a sharp sweep around the room with her hand. "The *person's* name is Taylor." She ran an angry hand through her shoulder-length hair. "Spoiler alert: Everyone is watching us. You can't be wailing like a baby kitten," she whispered, black and pink hair falling in front of her face.

Fernanda felt a wave of panic come over her, suddenly aware of how many seats seemed to be filled. "Your fault for calling me high," she shot back, voice not nearly as hushed as Taylor's was.

Taylor grabbed her arm and jerked her down the aisle to a seat towards the front. "I was not calling you high! Since me and my friends didn't know your name, we called you High Ponytail Girl."

Fernanda was less than pleased with this revelation. "I guess that's better than calling me high." She sat down in her seat and looked towards Taylor. "But I don't wear a high ponytail that often, do I?"

Taylor pointed a finger at her perfectly gelled head and at the curls cascading from the top of her head. "We could've called you Little Miss Gel Freak, but we didn't, did we?"

"Well, I could've called you…" Fernanda took a moment to examine the girl's features, her mind drawing a blank for a second. "Something that's too hurtful to put into words."

Taylor scoffed, hair whipping Fernanda in the face. "You can't find a thing wrong with me."

"You really wanna know what's wrong with you?" Fernanda grabbed a handful of Taylor's hair. "First off, your hair splits faster than your boyfriend did when you tried to kiss him." She dropped the hair and spat out, "And second off, I'd rather roll around in a dirty soccer field than hang out with your choice of *friends*." Fernanda thought Taylor would back down from that, but the girl got all up in her face, eyes radiant with hatred.

"I bet you want to roll around in a soccer field 'cause your little boyfriend is on the team, huh?"

Fernanda looked towards the stage and made a subtle pointing gesture. "Would you look at that? We're about to have a lecture." She made sure any hurt was wiped clear off her face. Not that there was any. She was completely over him anyhow. "Let's save the whining for later." She glanced back at Taylor for a split second. "Also, we were never dating. It was just a fling."

Taylor rolled her eyes and pulled out her phone. "You were the one who started the bitching," she whispered to herself, voice just barely loud enough for her companion to hear.

It worked, making Fernanda's head whip at Taylor. "Excuse me!" her voice inadvertently raised, making heads turn towards the pair again. "I clearly remember this starting with you."

"Me doing what?" Taylor shot back, completely forgetting the facade of being on her phone. "You were the one who assumed I was telling the whole world you were high!"

"Well, when you—" A loud sound echoed through the room from a microphone, making Fernanda pause. "If I could please have your attention?" a man said. Fernanda gulped and looked up at the stage, quite sure that those words were directed at her. The man onstage clapped his hands twice. "I'd like for us all to devote our attention to Queen Rajikumari to lead us through our anthem." He pressed a button on his podium, and the projection of their queen filled the air. Every person in the room readied themselves to rise from their seats, watching her watch them.

"All rise for your queen," she commanded. They obeyed. "All rise for the Raghunathan Collective Society, the RCS."

She placed her hand over her heart, covering her golden pin from view. "I hereby pledge to forever and always."

"I hereby pledge to forever and always," they all repeated in unison, arms limp by their sides.

The projection image changed to their flag, black and gold fabric shimmering together onstage. Queen Rajikumari's voice continued, "Devote all my support."

"Devote all my support." There was no hesitation as everyone filled the silence she created for them to fill.

The flag began to fade, and Queen Rajikumari's face filled the stage instead. "To our mighty leader." Her raven-colored lips formed the words slowly.

"To our mighty leader." Their voices went louder, anticipating the five most important words.

"Queen Rajikumari Raghunathan the Third." A look of pride filled her eyes as if she were really here in the room with them.

"Queen Rajikumari Raghunathan the Third," they finished. Their hands twitched at their sides, ready for her next command.

"Meus es in aeternum." The smallest twitch of satisfaction played on her lips. Her hands made a triangle over the pin on her chest, thumbs meeting together at the bottom. "RCS forever."

Their hands were more than ready, finally able to meet together in a show of strength. "RCS forever," they told her as her image faded from the screen.

Once the last glimpse of the queen was gone, the man who'd introduced her stepped up to the podium again. "My name is Mr. Bo Hunter, and I'm one of the leaders of the Raghunathan Collective Society Juvenile Security Program." He smiled at them, and Fernanda could feel the sunshine radiating from it. "Or the RCS-JSP. Long acronym, I know." That got a few chuckles from the crowd. "But I'll let you all in on a little secret." He looked side to side as if there might be something on the stage behind him. "Us officials just call it the JSP. We all know where we live, don't we?" More laughs erupted this time, which made him straighten up, grinning ear to ear. "But enough of that. You're here for the rules." He paused, taking a moment to stare them down with his dark blue eyes. "And the rules I shall give."

Fernanda looked from his face to her phone. He didn't have even half the stage presence that Queen Rajikumari had. "Is everyone with me?" he asked, hands clapping to an imaginary beat. "I'm not trying to repeat myself." Youch. Fernanda could hear the malice creeping into his voice, a smile starting to slip as he saw all the downward-facing heads. She put her phone down and looked up at him, gesturing for Taylor to do the same.

"You can't tell me what to do!" Taylor shot back in a low voice, refusing to stop scrolling.

"Rule number one!" Mr. Bo Hunter announced, a projection flashing his words. *All students get three meals a day at the appropriate time when we take the tests into account.* "I assume you all understand that we can't have a consistent time for each meal. Sometimes tests run long or end early, so we would hate to give you any food less than perfection." His malice was gone, finding some joy in explaining the rules. Adults always found comfort in rules.

Mr. Bo Hunter clicked the next button on the slide. "Rule number two." He clicked his tongue and let out a knowing chuckle. "Wake-up call is at 6:30, and lights out is at 9:45." He narrowed his eyes and looked out at the crowd as if knowing what they might be planning in their heads. "You sleep in your room and your room only. Nobody *sleeps together* if you catch my drift." He looked at them closely, like he was waiting for someone to break out in uncontrolled PDA right then and there. "We're almost halfway there," he encouraged, smile wide as ever. "Please, for the love of the RCS, stay off your phones!" Fernanda raised an eyebrow at her seatmate, and Taylor begrudgingly placed her phone in her pocket.

Another click sounded across the room. *Rule number three*, it read. *Always wear flexible clothing to tests. You never know what might happen.* "Another straightforward rule," he began, hand gesturing wildly toward the rules. "We just want to make sure you're able to do what we ask without having to worry about a shirt ripping or a dress flying up. Comfortable kids are the best kids."

Fernanda shared a look with the pink-haired firecracker. "And what is that supposed to mean?" Taylor mouthed towards her, slightly confused by his last words. Fernanda shrugged and turned back towards the man in question.

"We're halfway through!" Mr. Bo Hunter clapped his hands together thrice. "Time for rule number four." *Rule number four*, the holographic letters spelled out for them. *Never be late.* "This one's pretty serious," he told them, trying hard to make his smile go away. It twitched in the left corner of his mouth however. "Us leaders of the JSP care very much about punctuality. Tardiness, even by a second, could make or break a JSP mission." He pointed up at a clock in a corner of the big auditorium. "That's why we have clocks in every room. No excuse for being late if you know the time."

Fernanda felt someone poke her shoulder.

"Who was the one who told you we had to be early?" Taylor whisper-shouted at her. "Who saved your sorry ass today?"

Fernanda grimaced. "You did. Thanks for saving me, I guess." She sighed and said, "Sorry for saying that you groveled for Lizzie."

Taylor looked confused. "You never said that, did you?"

"Well, I implied it," Fernanda clarified, "so I'm apologizing for implying it."

Her roommate rolled her eyes. "I accept your apology."

Fernanda turned away from Taylor and turned back to the man on the stage. "Number five!" Mr. Bo Hunter's voice boomed, echoes filling the room. The words in the air changed, proclaiming *Rule number five: You can always stop.* "I know this might confuse you. Don't you always have to finish a test?" he laughed. It made Fernanda want to laugh and shiver at the same time. "But if you feel as though you can't go on, just let someone know. You won't get in trouble. We send all our proteges to a place of second chances: the Special Room." He waved dismissively at their questioning looks. "The Special Room is exactly what it seems. It's curated for you to have a unique second chance."

Well, that was a relief, Fernanda thought to herself. No need to be terribly stressed. "For rule number six," he continued, clicking the projector, "don't go into the basement." Murmurs of confusion were heard throughout the room. What was so bad about the basement? "Nothing is bad about the basement," Mr. Bo Hunter told them, as if reading Fernanda's mind. "We just don't allow kids to go down there. You will be dealt with if we catch you down there." Nobody really wanted to know what that entailed. "But wait!" He clapped his hands to silence them. "There's one more rule I forgot!" He looked over both shoulders. Mr. Bo Hunter clicked the projection remote once more. The crowd gasped in horror. Words dripping with something red hung in the air.

Rule number seven, the hologram announced.

RUN

RUN

RUN

A black paw print with a dripping red triangle inside it hung below the words, the symbol of the Black Claws taunting them. They all knew that it couldn't be blood, but it looked real enough to touch, real enough to be real.

Mr. Bo Hunter took one look at the message, and his eyes went to slits. The machine that was working the projections stood innocently in the corner. He strode over to it like a man on a mission. He raised his arm over it and brought it down with an inhuman speed. The projected words vanished, and the machine turned to a pile of dust, any trace of metal gone. He examined the small cut on his hand from smashing the machine, wiping it on his pants. "Well, that was certainly a surprise, wasn't it?" he asked the crowd. Nobody responded to him, but that was okay because he kept on going. "That was some more of their anti-queen propaganda. A whole pile of bullshit, that's what it is."

Fernanda shared a look with Taylor. Was an RCS-JSP official supposed to be swearing? But then again, it was the Black Claws who had just bombed their school and had now infiltrated the building.

"The audacity!" He paced the stage as if oblivious to the fact that he had a crowd of over a hundred and a room with an echo. "Is killing our children not enough? They have to strike fear into the ones who made it out alive? Try and take the confidence we're instilling in them?"

"Was this supposed to happen?" Taylor asked Fernanda, voice as light as a feather.

Fernanda gave her an eyeroll but said nothing, attention shooting back to Mr. Bo Hunter as he ranted on. "When did they get in?" His voice was more of a rushed, panicked muttering now, but it bounced around the room if you listened. "I've had this in my sight for the entire time! And there's no way they could've...oh." He looked at the crowd again as though his eyes had never left them. "I apologize for the interruption." His teeth gleamed a perfect white, and his cheeks flushed the right amount of scarlet. "Let me go on with rule number seven."

Hands moved to adjust his tie, the smallest drop of blood falling from the smallest scratch on his hand onto the smallest part of his golden tie. That dot infected the pristine goldenness that was so perfectly arranged on him, a disgusting rusty brown speck in the middle of a sea of perfect gold. As if knowing that, his non-bleeding hand grabbed the tie, suffocating the ugly speck. "Don't fail, my students." He squeezed the life out of the poor tie as he looked to his audience. "Don't fail."

His hand left the tie. The speck was now a blotch.

C HRISTINE WAS CONFUSED. THAT WAS the only word that came close to describing the blizzard of emotions that clouded her head. Just like last afternoon when rule number seven showed itself proudly in the air, she was confused. She wasn't scared like her roommate, Martha, had been when she shrieked at the blood-like words projected during their orientation. She wasn't frozen like the person to her left had been, his face contorting into a hideous shade of shock. She was just confused, just like she had been when the girl with the green braids had told her the fire had been started by a bomb. Not by a kid who had hypnotized them using his foolish display with the flames. Not by a match dropped into a vat of oily liquid.

She remembered that Mr. Bo Hunter had told the crowd they would have a test the next day. They'd be split into groups of three. Or maybe four. Her brain was having a hard time remembering exactly what he had told them. They were supposed to be doing a virtual reality (VR) simulation and acting out what a secret mission in enemy territory might look like without any of the real danger. High-stakes laser tag is what he had called it. One where they strapped you in a bulletproof harness with the laser gun attached (for show and not because there might be actual bullets) and placed a VR simulation device over your eyes. It wouldn't feel like a VR simulation like the simple ones you could play at the arcade or in your gaming room. Mr. Bo Hunter had shaken his head emphatically, knowing what they would go through. It would feel as real as the air and wind. Real as the wet leaves on the trees. You would easily forget that you were in a simulation.

And of course you weren't going to be sitting down or strapped to a seat. How would you get to simulate anything like that? The headset would be strapped tightly to your head, but not too tight. They were more like goggles anyway. You would forget that they were even there.

If your teammate fainted in the simulation, they fainted in real life. If you moved your right arm up in real life, it moved up in the simulation. If you jumped up onto a table in the simulation, you were jumping onto something similar in real life. But if you accidentally shot them, they were dead in the simulation but not in real life. It was slightly confusing to Christine. How could they mimic the simulation's surroundings in real life? But Mr. Bo Hunter told them not to worry about that part. They had that all figured out to a T. Mr. Bo Hunter promised it. He could promise anything.

The point of the simulation was that they wanted to see what their natural instincts were. That was what Mr. Bo Hunter said while his eyes bored into hers. They wanted to see how everyone would react to danger in a real mission. He cleared his throat before going over the four body responses people made on real missions.

Some froze. Their eyes would glaze over while their hands were on the trigger, stuck in slow motion. They would have that slack-jawed look of disbelief on their face as they let themselves stay in that position. Those people died quickly when a mission was compromised. All the enemy had to do was pull their trigger, and boom. They would be in a pool of blood, stuck in their last moments before death.

Some fled. They would desert their teammates as soon as they faced danger, leaving them to face the threat head on while they took the coward's way. Their actions always caught up to them however. In the rush to get away, they would trip an alarm or get shot down by a sniper. One moment, they were almost home free, and in the next, they were dead, their senses so focused on the exit that the bullets would get them.

Some fainted. Their hearts and heads would go into a panicked frenzy when an alarm would go off in the middle of an unwarranted search and seizure or when they were forced to stitch up a teammate for the continuation of a mission. They would let themselves fall limp against the dirt or the tiled floor instead of pushing through the wave of nausea and focusing. These people were the easiest targets, already in a state between consciousness and bliss, head flopped to the side and soul blinded by the stars. They would be shot in that perfect spot between the eyebrows. Dead as a doornail.

But the real ones, the ones who cared about the mission, the ones who were connected to their teammates, they would fight. They would fight to keep control of the situation, stepping up as the leader to guide their troops through. They would fight when the tides turned against them, shooting their guns when the enemy came at them. They would fight when all hope was lost, scraping and scratching till their soul carried them up into the stars, refusing to admit defeat until it chopped them at the neck.

The ones who could pass with flying colors were the ones who could make it to the Chair Room. The high-stakes laser tag was just the appetizer for the entree called the Chair Room. Inside, chairs lined up in perfect little rows. Left left, right right. Chairs lined up on the walls. Left left, right right. Chairs lined up on the ceiling. Left left, right right. You always wanted to make it to the Chair Room. That's where you were really tested. It wasn't as ominous as it sounded. Mr. Bo Hunter had reassured them with a megawatt smile. They were just chairs.

Chairs that crawled into your head.

Christine hadn't known where that thought came from, its voice twisting from somewhere deep in her fog of forgottenness. Chairs were just chairs. They could not walk and talk and crawl. They couldn't follow orders like a zombie. They just sat there. She didn't know anything about the chairs anyway. The RCS didn't just go around announcing what their secret tests for their JSP candidates were. She was nervous. Who wouldn't be nervous about being inside the Chair Room? But Mr. Bo Hunter was right. Chairs were just chairs.

Well, only the very cream of the crop passed that test, Mr. Bo Hunter had said while letting a light chuckle escape him. Only the very best made it to the grand finale. The Greats is what that lucky group of thirteen was called. They would be taken to the place where they would be pushed to the limit in the best (and only the best) way possible. The top ten would move on. They would be the next JSP agents and would get to protect the RCS and its queen from their enemies. And that was the end. Mr. Bo Hunter had told them all to leave and not be late for lunch, not even by a second.

Christine remembered walking from the orientation back to her room, Martha chattering nervously by her side. She had told Christine that tomorrow would be their day. Tomorrow, they would show all the JSP officials that they were special. Christine barely held back a chortle. She was pretty sure that seeing an imaginary fire start was not the kind of special thing they were looking for, but when it came to Queen Rajikumari, who knew? Who knew anything about anything when it came to the queen?

She had gone to bed, dinner of peas, chicken, and quinoa sitting in her stomach, waiting. She had gotten up from the bed to look out the window, hearing Martha's snores in the corner of the room. Looking down down down into the night, she felt her breathing stop. No streetlights, no car headlights, not even a lit-up window. Just an infinite abyss of night. The starless sky and the ground all looked the same, like an ocean when it was readying itself to sink a ship.

Christine had pushed her hands up to the glass, squishing her nose in the process. It was so perfect. So perfect out in the night sky that was everywhere. Unlike her, who thought she'd seen someone light a fire in front of her very eyes. Unlike her, who felt the flames twisting and jerking in the classroom, trying to fight its way over the desks to her. Unlike her, who would swear on her sanity that she'd been running away from the flaming hallways.

But she was wrong. Or so she'd been told. She had felt her futile frustration boiling up as she pushed her head up closer to the glass. The darkness never changed, never told her what she'd seen was wrong, never gave her the look that was reserved for *those people*. The ones who said their uncle was a certified zebra. The ones who said that said that the government was trying to poison them with sink faucets. And especially the ones who said that they saw the classroom light on fire when it never did.

But she wasn't them. She knew what she saw and saw what she knew. She saw the fire start. She knew the fire started. She saw the match and flame. She knew what fire looked like. She wasn't an idiot. But you didn't have to be an idiot to be one of them. She also knew that just as well.

Christine didn't like to be mushed in with *those people*. It made her feel like she was isolated from the normals, the people who knew it had been a bomb in the school. They would never believe her, having stuck a bright red warning siren on her head telling others to be careful because she never knew what was in front of her face anyhow. She saw the cuckoo signs people would do to each other while their eyes were on her because she wasn't like them at all. She was one of *those people*. She was crazy. Once you were crazy, you could never be normal. Not ever again.

You could jump. Jump, and all this would fade away.

It was like something had possessed her, dragging her arms to jerk open the floor-to-ceiling glass door. She hadn't even realized that it had led to a balcony until she felt the ground beneath her feet. Where would it all fade away to, she wondered to the thing, the thing that was heaving her feet up to the edge. What was it trying to make fade away? The darkness crawled up and down her spine peacefully, and she felt a distinct calm pass through her.

Maybe it went down forever. Maybe there was no ground here, just sky and air and ocean. That thing, the thing that liked to make her feel scared and safe at the same time, made her grip her fingers around the bars on the balcony. That thing tested the limits of the bars by hoisting her weight onto them a few times, toes leaving the ground by mere millimeters. It had yanked her over the edge, her butt landing on the top of the railing, feet kicking themselves in the darkness. She looked into that darkness, trying to see if there was anything, even just a flicker of light.

Nothing. Her right leg lifted up so it was almost parallel with her hip. Her toe had moved in the direction of the dark. Maybe she could go on forever. Maybe she could escape inside the dark. Maybe she'd be okay. Maybe, just maybe...

She awoke the next morning in her bed, the sun shining in her eyes from the window. Martha was still snoring, and the balcony door was latched shut. Christine had walked up towards it, seeing street lights and houses and cars. Her dreams were always vivid. She could remember them in excruciating detail when she awoke. But like all things that happened in that state between life and death, it was forgotten as the days rolled onward, lost to that forgotten space of things in her brain.

Breakfast had been good. Yogurt with granola and berries was a classic breakfast but filling. She had worn her lavender workout tank top with the criss-cross straps especially for this occasion, but a lady with the official JSP badge led her somewhere else. She remembered that for sure. The official said that she was too advanced for this little laser tag game, but she couldn't tell anyone that she hadn't done it. Instead, she would take a special test for a special person. The other candidates would be jealous, jealous that they weren't chosen for this special test and weren't led away to the Special Room.

Her last clear memory was the white walls and the wires. The room was a perfect white, the type that hurts your eyes to look at for too long. And the leopard. No one could forget about the stuffed leopard in that sea of white. Its glassy eyes looked right through her, as if she were just a ghost in its realm, wherever that might be.

The wires jumped from their spot on the counter, making her back away, butt landing on the bed with the parchment paper beneath it. The lights got brighter, and the bed vibrated with a steady pulsing rhythm that made her want to drift off and vomit at the same time. When the initial blinding subsided, she saw that the wires had woven themselves together in a crown of electrical snakes. It floated towards her, trying to bring her into its trap. Something deep inside her broke loose, coursing pure panic through her blood.

Christine scrambled away from the plastic nest of snakes, but the white walls grabbed her. It wrapped its white gloved hands around her midsection, holding her down. Her mouth poured out bloodcurdling screams along with a thick red liquid. Rivers of carmine poured from her mouth, leaking onto the white arms and the white gloves and the white walls. The crown of plastic wires landed on her head as the wall smashed a needle into her thigh.

Stars and pain. Pain and stars.

You could always stop, couldn't you? Mr. Bo Hunter had told them that. You could always stop no matter what. Screams so loud that they should have come to save her. They should have heard her. The white wall moved the light directly into her face, and her eyes went hazy. The screams stopped. Her throat went dry. So dry it couldn't form a sound. The white wall forced her mouth open, plastic gloves separating her pearly whites from each other. Things went through her mouth and down her throat.

The hands reached for the needle again. Screams again. Screams again and again and again. Christine kicked the white wall that reached for her, thrashing against the hold on her midsection and biting the hand that tried to pull her mouth apart. She felt the hands leave her midsection, her scarlet juices staining their whiteness. She felt the hands with the needle falter, afraid of giving up their own snow white perfection.

The buzzing started, the room swirling around her. Christine felt herself slump down to the side, head lolling at an unsightly angle. She knew she was gone, but she could still see them regaining their positions. They knew that they had control now, that they had the power. The needle pierced her flesh. Stars turned into darkness like that lucid dream she had the night before. They had won.

Again.

A noise. Quiet but raw. Painful but freeing. Christine could hear it slightly. It grew louder and louder as she got closer. Her eyes snapped open.

She was on fire. No, she could see herself on fire. She could hear someone laughing, and the noise was growing. She could feel the way her skin turned red and black. She could feel each pop when the little bubbles on her burst like soap. She could feel her skin curl and split and turn into dead skin. She could feel the exact moment when her head leaked the tomato-like substance. It dripped dripped dripped, drying instantly on the ashes that used to be silky black hair. Her head split gracefully down the middle, like a doctor had made a perfect line down the center.

It looked like a pot of soup. You had the rust-colored liquid boiling steadily when you stirred. You had the clumps of slimy things that were most likely edible, or that may have been the guts of an animal. And you had the black pepper you shook in with a heavy hand, making sure it was just the right amount of spicy. It looked delicious.

Except for the fact that it was inside her head.

The laughing turned into a choked cackling, and she wanted to go. Wanted to go away from this mess that may or may not have been happening. So she did.

Her eyes shut again. The noise went quieter. But the stars were back. Flashes of white light contorted her vision. She could feel the buzzing and the pain. So much pain.

Shriek. They should have heard her. They should have known she needed them. They promised to stop when it hurt.

They never did.

She wished she could go back into the darkness, but when her eyes opened, all she saw was light. Perfectly white light. Needles were everywhere. Two or three per hand. She shrieked. She was doused in her own ruby red soup. She wanted to stay in the dark forever.

And they were laughing. Laughing like an old man would laugh at an out-of-date joke. Laughing like a hyena that ate its child. Laughing like this was something they did on a normal basis. They weren't coming no matter how hard she screamed. They just laughed.

The stuffed leopard laughed too, shaking with convulsive giggles as it consumed her vision. It was terrifying how its eyes weren't vacant anymore, filling with a sick sort of liveliness as it opened its mouth and swallowed her.

Never trust the leopard.

Everything went blank. Like a teacher wiping down the whiteboard.

Swinging. Like a baby swinging on a cradle. Until a branch broke, and his neck snapped in half. Is that what happened to her? Had she fallen down a tree, or had the branch shaken and snapped in half? Shaking.

"Are you there?"

She opened her eyes to see Martha standing above her. Her confusion turned into relief. Christine ran a hand down the smooth material of her shirt.

"Thank Raji!" Martha said, running a hand through her hair. "You finally woke up!"

Christine looked at the time. 7:21 in the morning. "Is it time for the VR simulation now?" she asked with a half smile.

Martha looked at a booklet. Probably a schedule. "Yep, it's time for your group. Better get dressed right now. You barely have ten minutes."

Christine got up and went towards the mirror only to realize that she was already dressed when she saw her reflection. She supposed she must have forgotten that she slept in her workout clothes to preserve time in the morning. She turned to the bed, fluffing the pillows, stretching the blanket, and placing that leopard stuffie. Christine slipped on her shoes and walked out the door, ready for the day.

The door slammed shut. The lifeless eyes blinked. The leopard print laughed.

The VR simulation went great for Daisy. She passed the test with flying colors. It didn't go so great for her team however. They weren't quite sure who they were supposed to shoot as the enemies poured in. Their brains were overwhelmed from trying to differentiate the black and gold uniforms of their comrades from the black and red uniforms of their enemies. A team mission turned into a life-or-death solo mission within the first couple of minutes. She was pretty sure the rest of her teammates were sent home because of their flubs. The RCS would not accept that kind of stupidity into their JSP crew.

"Are you going to eat that stuffed pepper?"

Daisy rolled her eyes at her friend. "Yes, Ariella," she said while taking a comically large spoonful of whatever the stuffing might be. "I'm still going to eat my bell pepper."

Ariella ignored Daisy and turned to her own roommate and her half-eaten food with puppy eyes.

"Don't let her guilt you," Daisy called to the confused girl. "You need to fuel up for the next test."

Ariella shot Daisy a nasty glance. "We're about to go into the Chair Room in what? Ten minutes? I also need my food."

Daisy reluctantly passed the rest of her plate to Ariella. She was not the biggest fan of bell peppers anyway. "I thought you said we were going inside fifteen minutes early."

"I did." Ariella placed three spoons' worth of stuffing in her mouth. "About fwive minwutes ago."

Daisy was unamused by the food she saw falling from Ariella's mouth to her lap but said nothing.

"You'we not nerwvous about the Chaiw Woom, awre you?"

"For Raji's sake, Ariella. Chew then speak!" But yeah, she was nervous. It wasn't really about what the test was. It was about whether she would make it to the next round.

Ariella swallowed her food, making a satisfied *ahh* sound before repeating her question. "You sure you aren't feeling the teeniest bit nervous?"

"No." Daisy was not about to admit that it'd been eating away at her for a while now. "I just don't like bell peppers. You should know that."

Ariella cocked an eyebrow before letting out a snicker. "I wasn't talking about your food." She took another bite of stuffing, much smaller this time. "You look super nervous right now."

Daisy scoffed but said nothing in disagreement.

"Five-minute warning," the voice in the comms told them. "Start heading towards the Chair Room now."

Daisy barely heard Ariella moan in disappointment as she tried (and failed) to stuff the remaining pepper into her mouth. She followed the crowd down the narrow and twisting corridors. Her heart sped up as the what-ifs polluted her mind. She would be fine. She would go into the Chair Room with confidence and ace the test. They'd be in awe of how well she did, amazed someone could have results so good. She balled her hands into fists and slowly unfurled one finger at a time, counting down from ten in her head.

Ariella jogged slightly to catch up with her, all traces of food gone. "Are you ready for this? Being able to continue on our journey to get into the RCS security squad?"

"RCS-JSP," Daisy told her with a sigh. "Not whatever you just said."

"It's too many letters," Ariella said with a roll of her eyes. "And they all kind of sound the same."

"Three minutes left! Gather in a single file line outside of the Chair Room!" the voice told them over the intercom.

Daisy looked down at her hands, which had been furling and unfurling by themselves. Seven fingers were loose. Three were curled up. She couldn't decide if that was a good sign or not.

On one hand, she was aware of Ariella getting in line behind her, squeezing her shoulder slightly. On the other hand, she knew that she had nothing to worry about, that she could always stop if it was too much. But her brain was telling her about rule number seven. The fake red triangle dripping with fake red blood. The perfect black paw print. The richest ebony you'd ever laid eyes on. Why would the Black Claws tell them to run three times over if they hadn't meant it?

And that's when it was her turn to open the door to the Chair Room. She looked at the official standing outside the door, waiting for them to tell her what to do. They lowered their sunglasses from their eyes and winked at her, moving out of the way so she could turn the knob. "I'm supposed to open it?" Yeesh, she was scared, but that sounded slightly pathetic.

"Do you want to go into the Chair Room?" they asked her. She still wasn't quite sure if they were male or female. "Or do you not?"

She gave them an odd look. "I guess I do?"

They narrowed their eyes at her, and she realized one was blue and the other was brown. "No guesses. Just answers." Yet, they opened the door for her anyway. So she walked in.

For the first couple of seconds, her eyes were blinded by the onslaught of white light. Then, she saw it.

Chairs on the floor. Left left, right right.

Chairs on the walls. Left left, right right.

Chairs on the ceiling. Left left, right right.

That was why they called it the Chair Room. Mr. Bo Hunter wasn't kidding about how many chairs there were. Not in the least.

The room was big. Big enough that Daisy could, at the very least, fit her house in there. Maybe two of them. The walls were all black. Black as the panther that crawled around in the forest. The chairs, every single chair, were whiter than snow and had different numbers written along the sides. It looked like they were going to be experiments in a laboratory. Experiments seated in fancy looking recliner chairs. Each chair had a guide next to it, ready to lead you through your personalized journey. Daisy looked up and down and back and forth. The chairs and guides were in perfect rows like soldiers standing at attention.

"Daisy Brittany Pierre-Harper?" a lady's voice said.

Daisy looked to the left, trying to find the name that called her voice. "Left wall, Chair 224." She walked towards the wall and looked up, unsure of how she was supposed to reach the chair. "Walk up," the lady, who was presumably at Chair 224, said, hands gesturing for her to come forward.

Daisy fingered one of her green braids, scared of doing it the wrong way and being perceived as an idiot. "I don't know how to walk up a wall," she admitted, looking down at her dark blue athletic shoes. She was surprised that she wasn't more shocked about walking up walls. Daisy guessed that Mr. Bo Hunter's speech about the Chair Room had prepared her enough. "I've never had to do it before."

The woman laughed. Not a condescending laugh but a genuine one. "It's like walking on water," she told Daisy. "No one knows how until they do it."

Well, that didn't help much either, but she supposed they might be starting the test soon, and she'd be the only one not in her chair. "But I've never walked on water before," she murmured to herself. "No one has."

The lady up at Chair 224 heard her and shook her head with a knowing smile. "No has until they have to, Daisy."

She was a little surprised that the lady knew her name until she remembered that they had announced her name over the room. She looked at the left wall, at some of the kids already in their chairs, VR headsets strapped to them like brick goggles. Daisy closed her eyes and touched the wall with her hand, waiting for herself to have a sudden realization that she was now standing on the left wall.

"You can open your eyes now." The lady sounded bemused.

She did and realized she was doing a one-armed handstand on the wall. And it seemed that once she became aware she was in a one-armed handstand, she just had to fall in the most uncomfortable way possible. But she was on the left wall. And she was alive.

"Walk over to your chair, and then we'll get started," the lady told her.

Daisy got up hesitantly, afraid she'd lose her balance and tip back over onto the floor.

"You have to," the lady reminded her. "And if you have to, you always will."

She had to do this. Whether she fell off a million times and broke her skull in half or not, she had to. That thought, weird as it may have been, made her feel more confident. Her steps felt like the wrong kind of right, like an octopus trying to skip. Daisy began counting up and down with her fingers as a way to distract herself. "One, two, three, four, five…" She looked at her five fingers that were extended, then at the five fingers clenched in a fist. "Six, seven…"

Daisy arrived at her chair, and she felt the top of it looking down at her.

"Get in, Daisy. Get in the chair, and we'll begin."

Daisy barely heard the lady's voice as she moved towards the chair. She felt the smoothness of the faux leather beneath her fingers as she slowly lowered herself into its grasp. The chair was a lion's mouth, and it couldn't wait to swallow her. Daisy scrambled out of the chair. That was silly. Chairs could not roar. Chairs could not open their mouths. Chairs could not eat people.

They were just chairs. Nothing more.

"As entertaining as it is to see you panicking like this, I'd rather not see you free-fall off the wall from a lack of focus," the lady told her, eyes gesturing back towards Chair 224. "And almost everyone is situated."

Daisy laughed awkwardly, and they both knew she'd rather be at home than be here. She tried to do an aerobatic tumble of sorts onto the chair to show that she was not scared, thank you very much, and felt herself flying away. A hand wrapped around her arm and jerked her into the chair.

"And that," she heard the lady say, "is why we don't try to flip onto chairs. You almost fell right back onto the floor."

Daisy nodded, deciding that listening would probably be her best bet. Everyone had a limit.

"The constraints on your arms aren't here to detain you," the lady told her as metal constraints started wrapping around her arms on the armrests, like a lion pouncing on its prey. "They are there to make sure you don't rip off your VR headset if it becomes too much."

Well, if that wasn't ominous enough, Daisy wasn't sure what was. "And why might that not be a good idea?" she asked, voice pitching up slightly. Her arms struggled against the constraints, but the lion would not let go.

"The VR headset becomes one with your head to help the simulation become as immersive as possible, making sure it matches your exact brainwaves. I have to cut it off myself to make sure you don't end up with permanent brain damage from this. Does that make sense?"

A constraint wove its way around her waist, the coolness feeling like the last moments an antelope has before the lion kills it. "That's to make sure you don't fall off the wall. Sometimes, facing your deepest fears makes you get a little frenzied."

Daisy officially wanted out, and she said as such, but the lady gave her a look, pausing with the VR headset in her hands. Not a *I'm-so disappointed-in-you* look. Not even a *I-can't-believe-you-made-me-go-through-all-this-work-just-to-wuss-out* look. But a *I-wouldn't-do-that-if-I-were-you* look. Daisy looked at her again to make sure that she'd seen that right, but it was gone.

"I'll ask you once and once only, Daisy." The lady set her mouth into a firm line. "Do you want to go to the Special Room, or do you want to stay in the Chair Room?"

Daisy didn't like the way either of the rooms rolled off her tongue like complicated names of long-lost lizards. But at least she knew what was in the Chair Room. "I'd like to stay please," Daisy told her. "Thank you very much."

The lady didn't smile. She just nodded and placed the headset over Daisy's head, immersing her in darkness. "I want you to do two things and two things only."

Daisy waited, becoming unsettled with the darkness weaving around itself. It made the hairs on her arm rise.

"One: Always listen to my voice. Two: Don't *ever* stop."

And with that, Daisy felt herself falling and falling, vaguely remembering how Mr. Bo Hunter told them about rule number five, about how they could always stop. She landed in a maze. The lady didn't outright say *you're in a maze, find your way out*. But she could feel it all the same. Glass shards stuck out of the ground, taller than Daisy herself, and she supposed they were the walls of the maze. Everything around her was black except for the shards. They emitted light. She walked towards it, and the closer she got, the more the shards looked like enlarged crystals. Curious, she walked up to one, seeing her reflection in it. She had her box braids in, and she saw that they went down to her hips. She smiled. The other girl smiled back and swirled. The image shifted into a younger Daisy. A Daisy with beaded bracelets and braids. A Daisy with clear skin and tiny hands.

Watch this, she heard the lady's voice say from outside of her VR headset, and she realized that she must have done something right. **Close your eyes.**

She did, waiting for the command to open them again.

Open them.

Daisy did, and she saw she was in a kitchen, *her* kitchen, sitting at the table. Mom and JJ and Dad were all gathered around her. She knew she must have been younger because she still saw Dad there, and Mom was still called Mom and not Brittany. Her head moved down, and she saw a cake. A chocolate and vanilla cake to be exact. *Happy B-Day, Daisy*, it read.

You're double digits now! It was a memory, she concluded. A memory that was both painful and nostalgic at the same time. "Blow out the candles, Flower!" Mom said, sharing a look with Dad that could only be described as love. JJ clapped his hands together, and Daisy knew what came next. "Candelwes!" JJ said with a laugh. "Blwow blwow!" His hand waved around wildly, just missing the flames on her two candles. Dad grabbed him and hoisted him onto his hip, handing his camera to Mom.

"Three…"

Daisy grinned widely, looking from Mom to Dad in excitement.

"Two…"

She huffed an insanely large amount of air through her lips, cheeks puffed out to hold it.

"One!"

The flames went out, and the candles fell into the cake from the force of her breath. She heard cheering and clapping before she was back in front of the glass shard. Sure, it was a painful reminder of her last real birthday, but it was nice to remember. "Thanks," she whispered to whatever had taken her there. "I needed that."

Keep going.

It sounded like a queen echoing her command through the kingdom. She supposed the queen's wish was her command. She looked around and followed the path, waiting for another glass crystal to grab her attention, but none did. Emptiness just stretched out forever and ever. But she wasn't about to fail this test. She didn't like that look the lady gave her when she mentioned the Special Room.

Turn to the left. Pause.

Daisy did just that, looking at her reflection in the glass. It looked back at her and winked. She let out a scream, small and sharp, like a hook sinking itself into the throat of a fish. She watched the girl in the glass swirl around before grabbing her and dragging her through the crystal. As she was going through the crystal, her room and bed appeared in her vision. Daisy knew she wasn't at home, but it felt like she was. Her blanket wrapped around her, and her eyes opened like she'd just woken up. She took one glance at the calendar to her left before knowing exactly what memory she was in. Daisy leaped out of the covers but took care to smooth her blanket before leaving. Clad in her used-to-be-favorite cotton candy pajamas, she opened the door and traveled down the stairs.

JJ was on the last step, head leaning against the railing. When she took a closer look, she saw that he had fallen asleep with his pink stuffed bunny held tight in his grasp. Her feet moved forward past the scattered balloons and gifts in the living room. She peered around the entrance to the kitchen and saw her mom at the table, scissors in hand and paper snow falling around her. Daisy watched as her mom (unfortunately, she was still Mom here) grabbed the next piece of paper, which looked like it had something on it if she looked more closely. She felt sick to her stomach as her voice called out, "Mom?" Good Raji, that quiver in her voice sounded pathetic.

Her mom jumped like someone had shocked her with a full-force taser. "When did you wake up, Flower?"

Daisy looked at the snow that covered the underside of her mom's chair. "A couple of minutes ago." She moved her eyes to her mom's. "What are you doing?"

"Cutting paper," she said before going back to snipping.

Daisy walked closer and realized that it wasn't paper her mom was cutting. It was photos. Photos of their family on family trips. Photos of Daisy, her mom, and her dad at the hospital when she was born. Photos of their wedding with Daisy as the proud flower girl. "What are you doing?" She was horrified. Her mom was cutting up pure gold.

"I'm getting rid of Dad," ~~Mom~~ Brittany said, as if all moms did this every once in a while, tearing the family apart whenever life got a little too boring. "He left again last night." They both knew that was a boldfaced lie. Like Dad would willingly pack up the day before his son's birthday.

Daisy narrowed her eyes but said nothing. "What are we telling JJ?"

Brittany shrugged lazily as if matters like that were beneath her. "The truth. His dad packed up and ding-dong ditched us for his new fling."

That hit Daisy like a punch to the gut even though she had already lived this once before. "He's gone...like forever?"

The woman in the chair laughed as if Daisy's heartbroken expression was the funniest thing she'd ever seen. "Why else would I be chopping all this shit up? 'Cause I'm still hungover about him?"

Well, Daisy was sure about one thing. For her mom to be taking the news this well, she had to be a little hungover. "It's JJ's birthday," she told her mom seriously. "We are not telling him about Dad today."

And of course that's when the said person poked his head around the corner. "Dad's not hewre?"

She closed her eyes, mind already envisioning the answer she would give to JJ. But that answer never came. Her eyes opened, and she saw the glass shard and her plain old reflection again. "I didn't need to see that," she told the lady. "I didn't need to see that at all."

Yes, you did. That's the only way to get through.

She kept walking, but this time, a feeling of foreboding wrapped around her. Looking to the right, she saw a flash of Brittany screaming on the phone about the money her dad had "fucking promised to them." She looked to the left and saw her dad massaging his temples with Brittany standing over the broken lamp next to him, hate radiating from her eyes.

Daisy sped up through the glass maze, but the flashes turned to projections. The flashes she could deal with. They looked like movies you could see on your phone, unable to touch or reach you through the screen. But the projections? They looked like they could grab you, like they were looking into the very depths of her soul, and they frightened her. She recognized a scene of when JJ had told her how he hated Brittany. She fought through another scene when she caught her mom snipping her letters to her dad with her damned scissors.

She wanted out. She wanted to leave.

Daisy tried to tell herself that it was all fake, that she was just inside this stupid VR simulation while on a chair, but her brain wouldn't listen. Especially when she was forced to see the first time Dad had tried to bring his "fancy little bitch" to meet the kids. Wasn't that just a fun day.

The projections escalated, pure emotion leaking from them. Fury. Anguish. The feeling of pent-up screams that she could never ever let loose. It was too much, too much all at once. Brittany and JJ and Dad all screaming and yelling and throwing stuff everywhere. All of the bad memories. All of them at once.

All of this was your fault, Daisy. The words twisted around her like a black mist. *You should've been a better daughter. You should've kept the family together.*

The coolness of glass was beneath her hands, and she became aware that she was no longer running, no longer moving, just curled up in a ball of measly protection.

Get up. Get up and don't stop.

But she couldn't. Not with the memory of Brittany screaming at her about Dad. Not with all these projections of her worst days, all syncing up in a sick kind of harmony. "I want out," she whispered, her voice scratchy with despair. "I want to leave."

But the lady said nothing, probably trying to give her another chance.

Daisy looked at the projections around her, removed her arms from around her knees, and stood up. But that's when they shifted, becoming three tall shadows with horns and claws. She watched as they towered above her, pointing and whispering and cackling all at once.

You'll never keep the family together, Daisy. They all left.

The one behind her laughed louder, drowning out all the others with its shriek.

You're the reason they left. You didn't try hard enough.

All three crowded around her and crouched down to brush their claws against her braids. They all shook their heads in unison and screamed out their next words.

YOU'LL NEVER BE ENOUGH

The shadows laughed and laughed. Daisy heard them whisper and roar it over and over until it was all her head could process. She could never be enough. She would never be enough. Brittany and Dad and JJ never thought she was enough no matter how hard she tried.

That's why she couldn't keep Dad from running off to his new wife.

That's why she couldn't keep JJ engaged with the real world.

That's why she couldn't keep Mom from becoming Brittany.

She would never be enough. She would never keep them with her, could never make them love her the way she loved them. And that hurt. Bad.

And that's okay. You should never have to be enough.

The shadows shrank, their features morphing from being vague to more human-like. Their claws and horns shrank to become hands and hair. "I'll never be enough." Daisy's voice clawed its way out of her throat, coming out like a dying whisper. "But I don't have to be enough." The shadows screamed in pain, contorting in the strangest ways. The glass shards shattered into little pieces, popping the shadows and making them slowly change into piles of goo. The goo rose up in smoke and disappeared for good. That's when she knew it was over. "I want to leave now," she told the lady.

And leave you shall. Good job, Daisy. You deserve better.

She closed her eyes, feeling like she was at peace with herself for the first time in forever.

"I CAN'T BELIEVE THERE ARE ONLY thirteen kids left!" Carmen whispered in Kate's ear, who had passed the Chair Room test. "So many kids quit in there."

The Chair Room was a lot harder than Mr. Bo Hunter made it seem. Carmen refused to talk about what happened in that space between sleep and awareness, no matter how much anyone, especially Kate, pressed. She knew for a fact that the chair had crawled into her head and grabbed out her memories. It knew things that nobody else knew. It flaunted those painful moments over and over, making her crumble to the ground of that twisted glass maze.

But it was over, and she now knew what this next test was about. Kate told her that they would try to take her to a place, but as long as she followed the rules she laid out, she'd be okay. The only problem was that Kate hadn't outlined the rules, which meant that there was some kind of price attached. Kate loved prices.

Kate gave her a knowing look. "Thinking again?"

"Kinda," she admitted.

Kate nodded and raised an eyebrow. "Wanna know a secret?"

Carmen narrowed her eyes, mentally asking Kate the unspoken price on this so-called "gift." It was probably something related to an important rule for the test, but she didn't like the fact that Kate would have something over her. Hanging things over people's heads was *Carmen's* thing.

The kids walked to the next room. It was getting old. Scary room here, scary room there. Pick something new for Raji's sake. Carmen and Kate were at the back of the pack, and that was the perfect opportunity for Kate to bring up their dealings with each other. Carmen gave her gossip, and Kate gave her…hints.

"Think of it as an almost birthday gift. No strings attached."

"Not even a small one?" Carmen asked, twirling her hair. "Also, my birthday was months ago."

Kate placed her hands palms-up by her shoulders, ignoring the birthday comment. "Not even a small one. I can't tell you while we're in the testing room, but I can tell you out here."

Carmen was curious, and she hated that Kate could do that to her. She preferred to be in complete control of her emotions, ready to fake them at a moment's notice. But Kate could trigger her emotions without her realizing. And she knew it. "No one's stopping you from telling me," Carmen said in a hushed voice, lips moving minimally.

Kate tilted her head to the side. "Nobody's asking me to tell you either."

She hated Kate and her insane bantering skills. But if there was something Carmen hated more than getting her emotions triggered, it was losing, especially a game of words, and she'd already lost to Kai once. She didn't want to lose to Kate either. "Fine," she said, teeth clenched tight as can be.

"Fine what?"

Kate's smirk made Carmen want to slap her face silly. "Fine, you can tell me!" Carmen was glad she was talking quietly because her voice rose a little on the last three words.

"Say please." Kate patted Carmen's hair like an older sister patting her little sister's head patronizingly.

"Please fucking tell me before I blow your mouth off," Carmen demanded, slapping Kate's arm away.

Kate smoothly slid her arm around Carmen's shoulders, the affectionate move an excuse for her mouth to get close to her ear. "Don't repeat the chant. You can mouth it, but don't say it. That's how they get you."

And she was gone, skipping ahead like nothing had happened. Carmen wiped off any trace of annoyance and walked up to the group, mouth set into a determined line. As if Kate knew Carmen was a couple of paces behind her, she took a moment to turn around and wink. This time, Carmen had enough control to give her the nastiest glare imaginable, but Kate was unbothered. She turned into the only room with an open door. A sunglasses-wearing RCS-JSP official held it open. Stupid agents, always trying to hide their eyes from you.

Carmen flashed the official a fake grin as she walked into the dark room. It wasn't a large room per se, but it was big enough to comfortably house thirteen students and an official. It looked to be about the size of a normal living room, or maybe a bit bigger. The walls and floor were a deep burgundy. She guessed that this was the place where they'd make them do the chant. There was one white light in the very center of the floor.

She looked across the room towards Kate, who was at Christine's side like a leech. Christine was the girl who swore that their school caught on fire because of class shenanigans gone wrong. Everyone was aware of the greenhouse bomb. Carmen didn't know whose leg Christine wanted to pull with her stories.

Kate looked up and gave her the smallest of nods. Carmen wondered where she got her secret test info from, but the girl refused to tell her, using Carmen's signature grin on Carmen herself. She accepted it and milked as much as she could from her. So far, Carmen knew three things from Kate. One: Don't trust anybody high up. Two: The chairs crawl into your head. Three: Don't say the chant. Sure, that wasn't a lot, but that she was still here and not in the Special Room. She trusted Kate's info.

She looked at the light in the middle of the room, its unwavering strength scaring her. And nothing really scared her. Everyone gathered in a perfect circle around the light as if they needed it to keep them warm. "Look into the light," a JSP official said. Carmen turned towards the door and saw that it was closed. "Look deep into the light." Kate didn't say anything against looking into the light, so that must have been okay. It made her eyes go blind for a second. She started seeing different shades of red and yellow as if the sun was in front of her. "Don't stop looking. Open your eyes wider into the light." Carmen opened her eyes just a hint wider, and her eyes watered, the light twisting and swirling around to yellows and oranges. What were they trying to do? What was the light going to do to her? Looking at the brightness staring back at her, she could feel them trying to pull her in. They were trying to take her, to take them all, somewhere you were never supposed to go.

The light went out, and she could see things. She saw colors. Purple and gray and black. Those colors swirled around and around in her vision. She blinked, and after a few seconds, all she saw was a room with twelve people staring back at her. "Did you see those things? Did you see the colors and the lights?" Nobody responded, all staring into emptiness. All except Kate, who was mouthing something to her. Carmen squinted at her, willing herself to adjust to the dark and see Kate's lips more clearly. For life and death purposes only and not because she wanted to stare at Kate's lips.

"You can blink now," the official's voice said. Oops. Carmen had done that a while back. She saw everyone's gaze return to normal. Kate was still mouthing whatever she was trying to say to her. It looked like she was repeating the same word over and over.

"Say what I say when I say it. Do what I do when I do it." The white light was back, and in the middle was a hologram figure with the official's voice. The figure wore a robe of gold, and the robe's hood obscured their face. Carmen guessed that the hologram was speaking the official's words, most likely pre-recorded. The real-life official had moved to the corner, observing but not saying anything.

Ohh, Carmen mouthed at Kate, realizing she was trying to warn her about the chant.

"Exaudi vocem meam," the hologram said.

Everyone except Carmen and Kate repeated it, all voices morphing into one.

"Imitantur me." They moved their arms up and down, fingers outstretched like little five-legged spiders.

Carmen didn't like the way everyone's hands were in time, or the way her arms were getting tired of moving up and down, or the fact that nobody else seemed to be getting tired, not even Kate.

Teeth gleamed underneath the hood of their hologram leader, canines dripping down their face. "Da te mihi perpetuum."

Kate's eyes went wide with a hint of terror as everyone repeated the words. The official started doing some movements, and they all joined in, leaping laterally around the circle of light, arms still waving like lunatics. Carmen repeated the actions, watching as the people on either side of her grabbed her hands and fell backwards headfirst onto the floor, pulling her with them. She closed her eyes when they closed their eyes, welcoming the peaceful darkness that came when you closed your eyes. It helped her ignore the pain that came with throwing yourself onto the floor headfirst.

"Don't repeat me. Just listen now. Get up, open your eyes, and walk into the right wall."

They all got up, eyes bugging open in a way that could only be described as freaky, and walked into the right wall. Carmen followed the kid in front of her, definitely not because she forgot which side was right or left, but just to make sure she looked like she was placed under whatever spell everyone else was placed under.

Carmen didn't like the way the wall opened up like how a pond rippled when you skipped stones across its surface. It stopped rippling when she got through, as though the door to get back had shut. She really didn't like the way everyone disappeared once she stepped through the wall. She especially did not like the way it triggered a fear response in her, making her heart race and her breathing rocket out of control.

"Dimittis," the official whispered under their breath once the last person walked through the wall. "Donec ego dico aliter."

The walls were plastered in black and white spirals. Or was it actually white and black? Carmen walked around the room, but it felt more like a narrow hallway. When she moved forward, it was like she was wading through water. She could feel the liquid lapping around her knees, but she couldn't see it. When she looked down, only her legs and the floor stared back at her.

She closed her eyes, trying to calm herself down and make sense of what was happening at the same time. Across her eyelids, some text sprawled up. It was like someone had written across her eyelids, letting her know that they'd invaded her whether she let them or not.

Hello. I saw that you didn't obey the chant. Is that right?

What the fuck. She opened her eyes, but the words were now displayed across her line of sight, mocking her. "How do you know that?" she said aloud, putting up a brave front for whoever was there.

I know what you know. That's how :)

A chuckle echoed through the place. "What?"

They're trying to take you, but you didn't go.

Carmen felt a chill walk up and down her arms. The word "they're" echoed in her head. "You aren't them?" She didn't hear a response. Cupping her hands, she called out again. "Hello? You just planning on leaving me here?" But of course, whatever it was, said nothing back. She continued walking through the water she couldn't see, trying to get to the end of the spirals.

"Audisne me?"

She had no idea what it meant, but recognized the gibberish as sounding like the chant. She ignored it and kept going, legs marching her forward. She would get out of here whether or not that stupid voice came back.

"Audisne me?"

Carmen heard it again. The voice got louder, and it felt like the words were chasing her, trying to bind her to whatever they wanted her to be. She ran, flailing wildly through the invisible water. The random thought of her running from Middle-Aged Man back when she took the written test made her almost choke with hysterical laughter. She would not let them get her. She belonged to nobody but herself.

"Audisne me?"

The voice was mad. It was angry at her. It didn't like that she knew they were bad, that she was running away. It needed her to accept them. It needed her to repeat the words. That was how they got you. That was how they got them all.

The water rose up, cold waves engulfing her chest. She felt her feet leave the ground, and she somersaulted in the water. It was terrifying to be slowly sinking in a liquid you couldn't see, to know you had to reach the top but had no idea where the top might be. When her head finally broke the surface, she attempted to do some form of swimming, but it was slow. Too slow. The voice would catch her at this rate. They would get her. She could not let that happen.

Just as she struggled to swim another stroke, the purple and gray colors that she'd seen back in the chanting room wrapped around her again like a tornado. Her eyes blurred, and the water disappeared. She was sure that the whirlwind of colors was helping her mask from the voice. Within the whirlwind, she saw flashes, but it wasn't like the glass maze from the Chair Room. These were new. Things she'd never seen before. A girl made of red stole scarlet drops from her enemies. A girl made of green kneeled in the blackening woods, healing the trees. A girl made of fire burned a town with a smile. A girl made of lightning raised the dead, plants and people alike. A girl made of stripes and swirls made her enemies sleep and rise up as someone new. But that was nothing compared to the girl made of orange. She was like an asteroid flinging itself onto the earth, screaming like a devil, her enemies falling dead from her touch. Her eyes were the color of a deep orange clay. She was the one who scared Carmen, the one who was true evil.

This is a vision, Carmen. A vision of what is to come.

Carmen was pretty sure that all visions were of things that "were to come," but she said nothing of the sort. Instead, she watched as everything went away, and all she could see was the text scrawling in the air again.

I am not part of the RCS. I know that by showing you this, I'm giving you more questions than answers, but I thought it was better than being sent to where the others are.

She thought back to the chant and the way everyone had walked into the wall without question. "What am I supposed to do?" she asked. Carmen had no definite proof that the RCS was bad except for some bad feelings and cryptic words from Kate.

Wait. You'll know when it's time.

The mist swirled around again, and she closed her eyes, waiting till she felt nothing but her breath exiting her lungs to open them again. She was back in the chanting room with everyone else. This time, it looked like a normal room with a light on the ceiling and burgundy walls surrounding them. Everyone stood around chatting, maybe talking about their experience. Carmen took a moment to realize that there were only nine kids this time, ten if she counted herself.

The official began clapping, and all heads turned to Carmen and clapped too. "Looks like that's number ten, the last member we need for our team." The official smiled. No sunglasses. No hood. Their hair and eyes were brown with hints of red ombre peaking through their irises. "We now have the official members of the new Raghunathan Collective Society Juvenile Security Program. In order of who finished their test first, Christine Grayson, Ariella Bortell, and Taaj Karzin. Congratulations on being in the top three." They looked towards the next three. "Margaret Arlington, Daisy Pierre-Harper, and Kate Montoya. Great job being fourth, fifth, and sixth." Their eyes traveled towards the next group. "Fernanda López, Carson Schaffer, and Martha Skyevich. You all made it in time to be in seventh, eighth, and ninth place." All eyes turned to Carmen as she was the last person to return to the room. "And our grand number ten, our wild card, is Carmen Orlovski." Kate gave her a look that meant trouble from across the room as claps ricocheted around the walls. "All groups of three gather together. Number ten, come to me."

Carmen walked towards the official, eyes not-so-distinctly looking at Kate for help. She had nothing to say or was probably just scared of getting caught. Bitch. Carmen moved one foot in front of the other, stopping once she was almost nose-to-nose with the official. "I'm here."

They cocked their head to look up at Carmen, unafraid of being in the lesser position. "Good." Their tongue moved to and fro like a cobra. "You do know how to listen."

Well, that wasn't mysterious and freaky at all. "And?" She used her height to her advantage, towering over them.

"And that's good to know." They smiled at her before walking off and opening the door. "Everyone out. The final few have been chosen. Welcome to the RCS-JSP."

And that was the end of the trials.

It was awkward. That was the first thought that rocketed through Ariella's mind. Her second thought was that she really wanted to get out of the burgundy chanting room.

She tried thinking about something else, like what happened after the final test. The officials had called for a meeting. They told them they all did a good job before dealing them big news.

This was their new home. That shouldn't have been a big shock. They were official members of the RCS-JSP, but it hit hard. She wouldn't finish high school like the other kids. She wouldn't get to live in her house like other kids. She would be protecting the RCS. She would be considered a peer to all of the officials here. She wouldn't get to be a kid again.

The officials had also told the ten of them that they'd examined the results of all their tests, and they needed them all to do one last little thing. They were all on pins and needles because if that last test had been hard, nobody could imagine what this new thing might be.

The kids were led into a lab, and each person sat in a seat. They didn't look like chairs from the Chair Room. Just regular folding chairs, nothing out of the ordinary. They were being tested for one last thing. The officials seemed to take it seriously, giving each juvenile an injection. For what, they would not say. They then took a sample of blood from each one of them to run through tests.

The ten of them were all chattering like squirrels on caffeine after their test (more like a blood draw) was over, all back in the burgundy room. The officials told them that they would train in two groups of five: one group in the field and the other directing them over the comms. But first, the chosen ten would go home and pack up everything they needed to live at the RCS-JSP headquarters. And that's why she was here, stuck trying to "bond" with three girls she didn't know. Thank Raji that Daisy was also in her group, or she might have just blown a fuse.

"Let's go around and say our names in a circle," the one with the high ponytail said. "I'm Fernanda."

Daisy went next. "I'm Daisy."

Fernanda gave her a look. "I thought they called you Brittany in the Chair Room?"

Ariella inwardly sighed. That was not the question you asked Daisy when you first met her. Ariella should know. She made the same mistake in third grade.

"Some people have middle names," Daisy told Fernanda, sounding surprisingly neutral. "That's just my middle name."

Fernanda looked confused. "You can have a first name for a middle name?"

Youch. Ariella had no idea a vibe could get so awkward in a couple of quick seconds.

"Yep, next person," Daisy said.

The next person shot Daisy a glare before speaking. "I'm Christine."

She must have been *the* girl everyone was talking about, the one who really thought a guy set a room on fire at their school. This was going to be a fun group.

The girl with strikingly gray eyes went next, shifting her weight from one foot to the other. "I'm Carmen."

Fernanda's eyes narrowed at her. "You're Lizzie's friend, aren't you?"

Carmen gave her a smirk. "You're Jack's girl."

A low growl sounded in the room. "I am not, and you know it! You told Lizzie to get back with him!"

Carmen looked annoyed, arms crossed and face indignant. "I was the one who had to listen to him rant about how some girl broke up with him. Why would I tell him to break up with you?"

"Because you're best friends with Lizzie." She was practically vibrating with anger, and the rest of the girls were about to watch a catfight.

"I'm Ariella," she found herself blurting, unable to stand there and do nothing.

Fernanda flicked her eyes to Ariella and snorted. "Very clever, but I can fight for myself. Thank you very much."

Ariella narrowed her eyes at Fernanda, annoyed with her dismissive attitude. "Maybe I wasn't in the mood for a catfight."

Carmen whistled loudly, making the agitation on Fernanda's face much more clear. "Oh, I'm sorry." She didn't sound very sorry at all. "I didn't mean to start a fight that wasn't on your damn schedule."

Ariella hadn't been trying to add fuel to the fire, but watching the two girls fight when they were supposed to be "bonding" was also extremely awkward. "I personally don't want to watch my teammates fight." She took a moment to shrug dismissively. "But that's just my opinion. Not that it matters." Ariella noticed that the second group of five had stopped talking and were eying them suspiciously.

"Yeah." Fernanda put her hands on her hips, brown eyes glinting with something dangerous. "It doesn't." That's when Daisy had to speak up. "Her opinion matters. Thank you very much." Daisy never usually had this much spice, but she was glad for it.

A light chuckle escaped from Carmen's lips, enjoying their bickering. Ariella turned her attention to Carmen, refusing to let her stand outside of this mess she'd started. "It's not like you're any better," she trailed off, hoping someone would fill in the blanks for her.

"Yeah," Christine joined in. "You've been egging on Fernanda this whole time."

An official moved towards them, looking at their tight-lipped expressions. "Is everything going well?"

Fernanda wrapped her arm around the closest person next to her, who happened to be Daisy, and grinned. "It's going the best it could possibly go." When the official wasn't convinced, she went for drastic measures. "In fact," she grinned, "we're all having a team bonding sleepover when we go back to get to know each other a lot better."

The official's lip twitched into something of a knowing smile. "We can't wait to hear all about it."

That's how Ariella knew she was done for. She had not planned on spending her last weekend as a normal person at Fernanda's house. She wanted to have a quiet couple of days, draw in her room, talk with her parents, and just binge-watch a new show with Daisy. But Fernanda opened her fat mouth and screwed it up. "I never asked to spend a night at your house," Ariella said to the girl. "You're the last person I want to spend my weekend with."

"Relax." Fernanda said the two syllables like they were different words, patting Daisy's back before removing her hand. "You're not about to get killed at my house. I'm not a murderer."

Carmen looked up at the ceiling and clicked her tongue. "Says you," she whispered. Or it might've been something else, like "no one cares." She was good like that, making you think your mind was playing tricks on you. Carmen liked to mess with you. Ariella could tell from the twitch of her smirk when she'd started the fight with Fernanda.

Fernanda wasn't mad this time, or maybe this was what she looked like when she was even more mad. Ariella wasn't sure. Her face had the emptiest look except for her eyes, which looked like poisonous pools of mud. "If you want me to murder you, I don't have a problem with it."

Daisy stepped in between Fernanda and Carmen, sensing the tension that was brewing. That made Fernanda look at Ariella, eyes blazing. "I don't have a problem with murdering any one of you either," she clarified, in case anyone happened to wonder.

Daisy moved slightly in Ariella's direction as if deciding who she was ready to protect. Ariella appreciated that. She guessed that Carmen could protect herself with all the smirking she'd been doing.

"Let's not murder anyone right now," Christine told them, and Ariella gave a start. She'd completely forgotten that there were five of them. "We can worry about that when we all go back to the JSP headquarters." And the strange thing, the thing that made them all shiver, was that nobody could quite tell if she was kidding.

Fernanda cast Christine a grin. "I think I like this girl."

Ariella snorted as Daisy rolled her eyes. "Wouldn't have ever guessed." Her friend's emerald braids swayed as her head shook.

Carmen started walking away, calling over her shoulder as she went. "I gotta talk to Kate for a sec. Don't start a fight without me."

Christine's head shot up like a surprised marionette. "You're still friends with Kate?"

Carmen hesitated, her fingers twisting a blue and purple beaded bracelet around her wrist. "We're acquaintances," she said, like she was trying to find a better word for whatever either relationship might be. "She helps me, I help her."

Christine let loose a snort, making Fernanda cast a raised brow in her direction. "Looks like she can't make a lot of time for her real friends who almost died." Amusement colored her eyes. "But she sure has a lot of time for acquaintances."

Ariella did not like how this was going, but she wasn't sure what to say because they all knew Christine was lying. Or insane because nobody made up a crazy story about the school getting set on fire and tried to pass it as real for fun. There was also the fact that Ariella clearly remembered Kate hanging out with Christine for the whole week, but maybe when you were a little bit loopy, you couldn't remember that.

But Carmen didn't seem to know that you weren't supposed to mention any of that. Or maybe she did and wanted to stir the pot. Anything was possible with Carmen. "Maybe because you never almost died. Just a thought," she said before casting them a shrug before leaving them with a seething Christine. Carmen walked over to Kate, and both girls conversed in hushed tones.

Fernanda squinted at them and chuckled. "Guys," she said, eyes on the exchange between Carmen and Kate. "I think Carmen's a little flustered."

Ariella looked hard at the exchange going on and gasped along with Daisy. Christine didn't look amused, or maybe she'd already figured it out. Kate leaned in towards Carmen's ear, and Carmen had a touch of scarlet blooming across her cheeks. "It's probably from their close proximity. That's what Carmen's gonna say. I swear."

Fernanda shook her head. "Nah, she's too cool for that. She'll say something like she made herself blush to make Kate think that she was nervous."

They all giggled, and Fernanda looked very pleased with herself. "So, girls." She rubbed her hands together. "What are we planning for the sleepover? Going out?"

Ariella gave her an indignant look. "It's a sleepover. That means we stay in and sleep." The idea of going out with a group of girls like this scared her. "Right?"

Fernanda frowned. "Have you ever been to a sleepover?" When Ariella was about to speak up, she interrupted and amended her previous answer. "One with multiple girls?"

Ariella said nothing, and Fernanda gave her a smug look. "I thought so."

"She never actually said anything," Daisy tried to say, but she gave up when Fernanda let out a horse-worthy snort. "She's never been to a sleepover."

"Gee. Thanks, Daisy," Ariella snapped, but her voice didn't have much venom to it. "Why not just blurt out my deepest and darkest secrets while you're at it."

Fernanda clapped her hands together giddily, and Ariella was convinced that she might be a magician. No one should be able to change emotions that quickly. "Please do, Daisy! I'd love to hear about Ariella's secret past."

Daisy looked uncomfortable, afraid of messing up this very tentative peace. "Doubt Ariella even has an interesting past," she said dismissively. "She isn't super adventurous." Ariella had never been so grateful for an insult. Or was it more like a backhanded compliment?

"Those are the people with the most drama. Even an idiot knows that." Nobody was sure who she was referring to as the idiot.

Christine bristled and looked towards Ariella to say the proper words in this situation. But this was a person with clear insanity. Would they be considered an idiot? "Nobody's an idiot here," she decided to say. To distract Christine from the fact that she didn't explicitly name her, she added, "Even you, Fernanda."

Fernanda's face turned the color of a blushing fox, and Ariella was concerned (only for half a second) that she might be choking.

"I'm back," Carmen announced, hands in the air, as if they would rush to her like a wife when her husband comes back from war. "Did ya miss me?"

"Not especially," Fernanda said, putting Ariella's thoughts into words. "But I think Kate might."

To Ariella's surprise, Carmen scrunched her face up into an expression of utmost confusion. "And why would she miss me?"

Christine coughed loudly. They all looked to her, and she looked right back. "My throat tickled," she explained, in case they were waiting for her to drop some super secret piece of news. "Does someone have a cough drop?"

Daisy clicked her tongue and let out a sigh. "I have some back in my room…"

The whole conversation stopped there, and Ariella thought that running out of the room might just be a good idea. She thought the arguing had been tense, but this silence was even worse. It always sucked when conversations reached an awkward lull. If she ran out, Daisy would at least have an excuse to escape too, but she remembered that Christine was supposed to be the crazy one and decided against it.

It was so quiet that she was actually able to hear a clock ticking in the corner. Ariella eyed Daisy from across the room, trying to communicate with her eyes. *Tell them you have to use the bathroom*, she tried to say. *I'll follow you out.*

Daisy seemed to be off her look-reading game today because her eyes said nothing back. She didn't even make a small nod in response to Ariella's plan. Carmen clapped her hands once and chuckled. "So are we doing this sleepover or what?"

Fernanda's eyes lazily glanced in Carmen's direction, as though she couldn't be bothered to look her in the eyes. "We're doing something low-key at my house since she…" Fernanda just had to narrow her eyes and point her finger at Ariella before continuing, "Doesn't like to party."

Carmen made a face at Ariella, and she felt herself shrink. "I guess that's fine. Whose house is the party going to be at?"

Fernanda shrugged. "Does it really matter?"

Christine suddenly raised her hand, and they all looked at her. "I don't think I can go."

Fernanda sighed sharply, and Ariella winced for Christine. "And why can't you go? I thought we agreed to let our problems be until we came back."

"My parents." Christine's left thumb traced an indecipherable pattern around her pointer finger. "They don't let me sleep over at other people's places, and they're going to want me to stay home for the next couple of days."

Daisy held up her hand, stopping Fernanda from going off on another angry tangent. "That's fine. It'll be just us four."

The official's voice boomed across the room, "Alright, kids! Start packing up. We'll see you on Monday." A pause. "Enjoy your last weekend being normal."

IT WAS THE SECOND-TO-LAST DAY before they were set to return to the RCS-JSP headquarters. Daisy, Ariella, and Fernanda were all in Fernanda's room, waiting for Carmen to arrive so the actual fun could start.

"I'm so fucking annoyed right now!" Fernanda said aloud, hanging upside down off her bed, head grazing the carpet. She waited for a response. Daisy gave her a sideways glance. Ariella didn't even glance up from scrolling on Daisy's phone. Fernanda bothered herself to look at them. "You're supposed to ask what's wrong."

Daisy turned her head fully to look over at Fernanda, sighing as she asked, "Well, what's wrong?"

Fernanda only sighed deeper, trying to add a dramatic silence to the moment. "It's okay. I don't have to tell you." She shook her head. "It's not that important anyway."

Daisy was now invested, and Fernanda felt her spirits lift slightly. "No, I'm sure it is, Fernanda. Maybe I can help."

Fernanda made a face like she was thinking about it (even though she knew exactly what her problem was) before

Ariella said, without bothering to move her eyes, "It's about James, isn't it?"

Fernanda gave the back of her head a nasty look. "His name is Jack, but yeah, him."

"Well, you either like him or you don't. There isn't any need to go all back and forth," Ariella said, stating what seemed to be obvious to her.

Figures. That girl had been making goo-goo eyes at her brother when they were eating dinner downstairs. Fernanda decided to say just as much, tossing a pillow at her while saying, "Says the girl whose only crush is my ugly-ass brother."

Ariella dropped Daisy's phone and proceeded to slam the pillow into Fernanda's face. "What the heck? I most absolutely do not!"

Daisy added in her two cents, "Don't worry. I already knew." Fernanda gave her a murderous look as she continued, "Fernanda told me when she saw the eye flirting."

Ariella and Daisy seemed to have a private conversation with their eyes before the former launched a pillow at Daisy, knocking her clear onto her back. "You promised not to tell!"

Fernanda also felt a silk encasing of fake feathers meeting her head. "What are you? A stalker?" Ariella yelled, attempting to murder her with pillows.

Fernanda picked up the pillow Ariella had somehow gotten from the bed and retaliated, leaping off the bed and hitting her guest square in the jaw. A full-out fight ensued until the door slowly creaked open, but Fernanda was oblivious until the person at the door called her name. "Nanda?" Turning to look at her brother, Fernanda snatched Ariella's pillow, which had been smacking her in the face for a little bit, and tossed it at him. He caught it midair, which only angered her more. "Fuck off, Carlos!"

Carlos raised his hands. "Nanda, calm down. I only came up to tell you someone's at the door."

Fernanda leaped up and shoved him out the door. "Let them in, you idiot! It's like below freezing right now!"

Carlos gave Ariella a look that probably said *isn't-she-just-so-annoying* before following his sister out. Ariella chuckled.

Fernanda slid down the banister to the front door. When she opened the door, Carmen stood there in a strapless scarlet top, a black leather mini skirt, and bulky combat boots. The top had to have a corset. There was no way her body was so perfect on its own, Fernanda thought. She had to admit it. Carmen knew how to style herself.

"Welcome, I guess," Fernanda said, letting her into the house. "Everyone's upstairs."

Carmen took off her boots before hopping up the stairs two at a time. "Thanks for the warm welcome, Nanda."

That made Fernanda grit her teeth in annoyance. She really hated when other people tried to shorten her name. Fernanda saw Carmen leaning her ear against the bedroom door, listening in to whatever was being said on the other side. "What's going—" She was cut off by Carmen placing a finger over her lips and gesturing at the door.

Fernanda put her ear up to the door and heard someone say, "What are we doing today anyway? Watching a movie or something?" That had to be Ariella.

A long, awkward pause. "She didn't tell you?"

"Tell me what?"

Fernanda was suddenly very glad that she wasn't in the room.

"The plan for tonight," Daisy said, her voice getting louder as she walked closer to the door. "She told me that she told you."

Ariella seemed to scoff before asking, "Well, what's the plan?"

Daisy's voice dropped, as though she were afraid of someone overhearing. Both girls pressed their ears closer to the door. "You know Lizzie Theibes, right?"

"You mean Jack's girl?" Ariella let out a loud sigh like she knew where this conversation was going.

Daisy chuckled. "They broke up."

"Again?" Ariella seemed more annoyed than surprised.

Carmen took that moment to open the door and strut into the room, dragging a very apprehensive Fernanda behind her. "You ladies ready to par-tay?"

Dead quiet filled the air, and Ariella took a stab at it. "So… this isn't a chill hangout kinda sleepover?"

Fernanda shrugged sheepishly, trying to think of some kind of excuse. "I mean, I guess plans change, ya know," she began, trying to make her escape out of the room.

Everyone else followed her down the spiral staircase and into the kitchen, which had one of the highest ceilings some of them had ever seen in a house. Ariella looked at the chandelier that was smack dab in the middle of the room. "Well, whose house is it at? Christine's?"

Daisy gave her a look. Fernanda began nervously rubbing the back of her head. "No, Christine's busy. Remember?" That last word had more bite than was probably necessary, but Fernanda couldn't care less. Ariella gestured for her to continue, and Fernanda reluctantly did. "It's at Lizzie's house."

"And you're invited?" Ariella asked condescendingly.

"Ouch," Carmen murmured, tossing Fernanda a sympathetic glance.

Fernanda huffed and busied herself with pouring some chips into a bowl. How dare Ariella poke fun at her? She'd better believe that they had a *large* assortment of knives in the kitchen. "What are we in? Sixth grade?" She opened another bag of chips and said, "It's an open house party for sophomores only. No invites needed."

Ariella gestured to her comfy sweats and oversized shirt that had the words *Don't Talk To Me Without My Coffee*. Fernanda thought that the first four words on the shirt did a splendid job of summing her up as a person. "You expect me to go to my very first party of the year in this?" She was pretty sure this was Ariella's first party, period, but she was polite and said nothing of the sort.

Carmen gave Fernanda a confused look, eyes gesturing toward Daisy and Ariella. "Wait, why didn't you tell her about the plan?"

Fernanda began grabbing cans of soda out of the fridge and setting them out, trying to keep her hands moving. It was hard to sit still when you had three strangers inside your house, two of whom you'd rather leave outside. "I told Daisy the plan. I just knew that if I told Ariella, she wouldn't come."

Carmen sighed, pinching the bridge of her nose. "Well, you could have at least told me you weren't telling Ariella the plan! I would've brought her something to wear."

Fernanda shrugged and opened a can of soda, taking a large gulp of the sugary brown liquid. It had the pleasant burn that came with drinking too much in one gulp. "She can borrow something from me, and don't worry about Daisy. She has her stuff in her bag."

Ariella crossed her arms and huffed. "I'm not going to a party. You all know how antisocial I am by now! I'll make a huge fool of myself." She locked eyes with Fernanda for a brief moment.

"Well, since it's Lizzie's party, everyone will probably get drunk," Carmen said, trying to comfort Ariella. "Nobody will remember you making a fool of yourself."

"I don't wanna get drunk!" Ariella whined, a bit of terror creeping into her voice.

"You're a pain sometimes, Ariella. You know that, right?" Fernanda said, crunching the soda can up in her hand. It made a cut on her palm, and she hissed out a couple of unsavory words under her breath. She went to the fridge and pulled out a Red Paw drink.

"I don't think caffeine mixes well with alcohol," Ariella stated.

Fernanda rolled her eyes at the girl, but Daisy said, "Ya know, she's probably right."

"Fine. I'll just put it back." She opened the fridge and threw the drink back in. "Happy?"

"That I may have saved a life? Maybe not," Ariella said.

This girl was insufferable. She was seriously considering dropping out of the JSP if this person had to be in her group. "Keep this up, and you'll have to go to the party in those sweats," Fernanda threatened.

Carmen looked between them and leaned over toward Daisy. "What's got them so riled up?"

Daisy sighed and rolled her eyes. "Fernanda did tell you why she wants to go to the party, right?"

Carmen shrugged. "She said it was the first good party of the year, and she's still pissed at Jack, so…ya know."

Daisy shook her head. "You know Lizzie was Jack's *other girl* for like forever."

"And Fernanda has been Jack's *other other girl* for like forever," Ariella piped up.

Fernanda tried tossing an empty chip bag at Ariella, but it floated limply to the floor. Ariella snorted but said nothing. Daisy glanced over to the other two girls and then back to Carmen, waiting for the impending blowup about to happen.

"No, Jack and Lizzie stopped talking," Fernanda said, grabbing her soda and taking a well-deserved sip. "Jack is obviously going to Lizzie's party..."

Carmen's mouth opened in shock. A small smirk appeared on her face. "Damn, the girl's got game. I'll give you that much."

Fernanda glanced at the empty chip bag on the floor and the piles of crumbs on the counter. She would have to rope Carlos into cleaning the kitchen somehow. There was no way she was doing it herself.

"Since when is pining over the same guy after he repeatedly says he doesn't like you considered game? That's desperation," Ariella said.

Fernanda's hand was poised in the air, halfway to Ariella's face before she stopped herself. She decided to respond with words instead. "How dare you?! He actually asked me out, but I declined," Fernanda said, wishing the words back into her mouth as soon as she said it. Maybe it would've been better to slap her.

"HE WHAT?!" all three girls screamed at once.

"He asked me out while we were at the JSP headquarters," Fernanda mumbled, all her bravado disappearing. "Over text."

"While he was still talking with Lizzie?!" Carmen asked, trying to piece a timeline together.

"No, he wasn't talking with Lizzie, right? It was right after Lizzie threw the chocolates down the toilet. Right, Fernanda?" Daisy exclaimed. Fernanda wondered where she would have gotten such information.

Ariella sighed and shook her head sadly. "The guy's such a player. How does he even still get girls at this point?"

"He's hot," Carmen said, stating the obvious. "To the majority of the population at least."

Fernanda shot Carmen a dirty look. "Hey, he's definitely not my type," Carmen told her, hands raised in the air. "You can keep your player."

"He's not a player," Fernanda muttered under her breath.

"But you did call him a bitch like twenty times in the car ride home," Ariella stated blankly.

"That was the car ride," Fernanda insisted. "This is a weekend party, which is two different things."

"Oh, so you made up this week?" Ariella asked.

"Heck no!" Fernanda exclaimed. "But that doesn't mean I don't want to."

At that exact moment, Carlos peeked his head inside the kitchen. "Can you guys be any louder?"

Fernanda flipped him off. "Out! Now! Go back to your room and shoot someone in your VR game."

"Geez, Nanda. I just wanted some food. The kitchen isn't yours, ya know," Carlos said, grabbing the carefully poured bowl of chips. He paused, and his gaze landed on Carmen, taking in her sparkly red top. "What kinda sleepover is this?"

Carmen spun on the toe of her sneaker, clearly soaking up the attention. "The fun kind," she answered with a wink toward him.

Ariella gave the back of her head a warning glance before saying, "They wanna go party at Lizzie's." She reached for a chip from Carlos's bowl, and he held it out to her.

Carlos turned his attention back to his little sister. "Is she serious right now? Do you know what Mom would say if she found out about this little *adventure* you're planning?"

Before Fernanda could mention all the times she'd been blackmailed into covering for his little *adventures*, Ariella gave Carlos her best innocent doe-eyed look and said, "That's why we need you to cover for us because it's not a party we can skip." She had to keep herself from laughing because who really believed that Ariella was a party girl?

Apparently, Carlos did because his face changed, and he focused on his sister, avoiding Ariella's gaze. "But I don't want to get in trouble for something you all did. That's not my problem."

Ariella smiled up at him and tried her best to casually bump her hip against his. Spoiler alert: It looked awkward. "It's the first party of the year. I promise we'll be back before midnight. Right, Fernanda?"

Fernanda morphed her face from one of hysterical laughter to a simple nod. "Ye-yeah, midnight's the latest we'll be out."

Carlos looked at Ariella and sighed, throwing his one free hand up in the air as he walked out. "Whatever, but if you're back any later, I'm not holding back."

Once he was out of the room, Ariella looked pointedly at Fernanda. "You're *welcome*."

Carmen whistled through her teeth, eyes merry with mischief. "Damn, Ariella. Didn't think you had it in you. Our little girl is growing up!"

Ariella blushed as she brushed a lock of her hair behind her ear. "Someone had to think of the logistical side of the operation."

Fernanda's face slowly stretched into a large grin. "I told you all she'd come around to the idea!" she exclaimed, hoping that this could join them on the same side.

Daisy gave her a look of disbelief, seeing straight through her BS. "Actually, you only told me."

"Just because I got us an alibi doesn't mean I like the reason we're going," Ariella said while looking at Fernanda. "I actually still hate the idea of you with Jack. He's a player."

"Is not!" Fernanda huffed indignantly. "He's just..."

"A bitch?" Carmen asked.

"An asshole?" Daisy offered.

"Annoying sometimes. But yeah, also all those things too," Fernanda admitted.

"And you still like him?" Ariella asked in slight disbelief, wondering how she saw past any of that.

"Forget that!" Daisy said, not wanting to veer away too much from what had been happening previously. "Let's try and keep whatever fragile peace we have now."

There was a pause before Ariella made a gesture towards her outfit. "Are we getting ready to go to Lizzie's party or what?" she asked. "I don't really want to show up in sweats."

Fernanda nodded, walking up the steps two at a time. "But we can't show up early because it seems like we have nothing better to do. We'll come like an hour or two after the start. Does that sound good?"

Carmen raised her hand and said, "Are we planning on walking a mile or two to the party? It's freezing out there!"

Fernanda stopped, chiding herself for being so stupid while slapping her hand against her forehead. "Shoot, don't think I thought that through. We could ask for a ride..."

"But Carlos is our alibi!" Ariella shot back, knowing where this was going. "I really don't want to feel the wrath of your parents."

Fernanda sighed, leaning on the stairwell. Ariella had a point. No one really wanted to feel the full wrath of Mr. and Mrs. López. "Erm, I guess we're walking over?"

Carmen smirked, and the girls knew she had an idea. Whether the idea was plausible was still up in the air. "What if we take one of your parents' cars? I do have my driving license."

Daisy and Ariella's eyes met, and Fernanda knew that they were not willing to go to such lengths for a party. "Well—" Daisy tried, but she was quickly cut off by Fernanda leaping up and almost tripping over something invisible to the rest of them.

"Let's take Carlos's car! He has a really nice car. Got it for having good behavior or something." Fernanda rolled her eyes at the last bit because he got a new car while she had to get her parents' old car just because she was one year younger. She rushed into her room to find something suitable for Ariella. The conversation continued downstairs, and Fernanda did her best to listen in.

"As long as we don't crash it, I don't care." That was presumably Carmen.

Fernanda heard a gagging sound. Daisy said, "Don't say that, or we'll crash."

Ariella was about to respond, but she was cut off by having a pair of jean shorts thrown into her face. "Put that on," Fernanda demanded. If she was about to fork over an outfit to Ariella, you'd better believe it'd be a damn good one. "I think we're about the same size anyway."

"On the stairs?" Ariella asked incredulously.

"Of course not, stupid. Get into my room or the bathroom and put them on. I'll find a shirt," Fernanda said, rushing back into her room. The rest of the girls followed her.

"But why am I wearing shorts if Carmen's wearing a skirt?" Ariella asked.

Fernanda sighed, annoyed again. How was she supposed to survive the rest of her life with this girl as her teammate?

"If you wear a skirt like Carmen, you'll stand out like her. You'll thank me for this, especially once you get drunk."

"I'm not drinking!" Ariella said, crossing her arms. "I don't want to get in trouble in case we get busted."

Carmen burst out laughing, and Fernanda joined in, both girls collapsing on the bed in hysterical laughter. Daisy only shook her head at their overly dramatic performance. She looked at Ariella's overly innocent and confused look and almost burst out laughing herself. Almost but not quite. She smiled instead, jutting her thumb at the two girls who were red from laughing. "If the RCS officials come, everyone's pretty much screwed whether you're drunk or not. If you don't want to get caught, don't come."

Ariella sighed. "Guess I'm in over my head now." She looked at Fernanda and Carmen, who were still torn to shreds about her innocence.

"Go find me a shirt!" she said, kicking at Fernanda. It took a moment, but she complied, wiping one last tear from her eye as she finally began rooting around her closet for a shirt. "Do you want it to blend in or pop?"

"I think I'm fine with it being a little more casual," Ariella admitted. "I'm not Carmen."

Carmen twirled in front of the mirror and winked at her reflection. "Can't have two of me now, can we?"

Daisy sucked in her breath through her teeth and shook her head. "That'd be a nightmare." Carmen shot her a nasty look through the mirror.

Fernanda pulled out a black top with one strap on the left side. It was silky and cropped but had a very simplistic design. "Would this do? Seems like your vibe, right?"

Ariella held up her ballerina blue jean shorts that Fernanda had handed her before. "Do you have a white jean skort instead since it has shorts built into it? I promise not to spill anything on it!"

Fernanda sighed, pulling out a wrinkled skort. She didn't really like the color white, especially when the risk of spilling something on her grew. And let's be honest, tipsy people do not have the best balance. "I haven't worn it in a little while, so it's a bit wrinkled."

Ariella gestured out of the room. "I'll be changing in the bathroom."

"Okay, Daisy and I will change in my room."

But once she came back, it was clear she was uncomfortable with her outfit. "Fernanda, do you have something a little less revealing?"

Fernanda waved her worries off with the flick of a wrist. "But you look so cute! Perfect for a party of Lizzie's."

Carmen nodded, eyeing her up and down critically. "I mean, compared to the other girls, I'd say you're pretty covered up."

Ariella gestured to the skirt that was hiking up her upper thigh. "What if I have to bend over? Or want to sit down? This isn't covering a thing."

Carmen held up a fist. "That's why you have these. Clock 'em if they get a little *too* enthusiastic."

Ariella looked dubious. "Have you ever had to clock someone 'cause they weren't listening?"

"Not recently," Carmen decided to say, and Fernanda was pretty sure this was the closest to the truth that they'd get.

Ariella's eyes widened. "I can't punch someone to save my life!" She paused, raising an eyebrow. "When did you have to punch a guy?"

Fernanda groaned as she began picking out her outfit. "That's enough, Carmen," she said with a pointed look toward the girl. "We still need her to come to the party with us."

Carmen flinched when she said that, as if the words had surprised her. "Yeah, don't worry about it, Ariella. We'll be here."

Ariella looked down at her outfit and shook her head. "How about I keep the shirt and just wear jeans? Like straight-legged white jeans?"

Fernanda said, "Sure, if that makes you happy. They should be toward the bottom."

Ariella happily began looking through the closet, and Fernanda held up her own outfit: a faded blue denim tube top and a beige miniskirt covered with fringe. "How do we feel about this, girls? Yay or nay?"

"I love it!" Carmen exclaimed, jumping up and down in excitement.

Daisy nodded her approval. "It looks party appropriate."

Ariella, however, gave her reservations about the outfit. "Appropriate is about the last word I'd use to describe that outfit, but I think you'll look good." She grabbed her white jeans and walked back to the bathroom.

"What time is it?" Daisy asked, trying to break the unexpected stillness that Ariella's leaving brought.

Carmen looked at her phone. "6:37. We need to go in about ninety minutes."

Daisy nodded as she began changing into her outfit: a simple pale green mini dress held up with a noticeable but not overly large bow that was tied around her neck. It didn't match her braids exactly (obviously), but it still looked perfect together in a way. "Should I wear sneakers or boots?" she asked Carmen, who was reapplying her lipstick.

Carmen looked over and nodded her approval to the sneakers. "I think you value comfort over being cutesy. Plus, that dress is gorge, Daisy!"

Daisy smiled and did a little twirl.

Fernanda looked up from changing into her outfit. "That's beautiful!"

Daisy gestured to both of the girls. "You too, girls! I could never pull off looks like that."

Carmen puckered her lips in the mirror and nodded. "Yeah, this look is strictly me." They all chuckled, knowing what she said was true.

Ariella came back into the room, wearing the white jeans. "I feel so much better in this. Thanks, Fernanda."

"Whatever floats your boat," Fernanda said back.

Ariella saw Daisy, and her eyes went wide with surprise. "That's fu-reaking beautiful! I love it!"

Daisy blushed, not used to having all eyes on her. "Thanks. Glad you all like it."

Carmen glanced at her phone and said, "Do we wanna watch a movie while doing each other's makeup? We still have time to kill."

Fernanda looked at Ariella before sprinting down the stairs, the other girl quickly racing to get ahead. "Dibs on picking the movie!" Fernanda yelled.

"We are not watching *Joana's Body*! I don't care how hot you think Milan Focks is!" Ariella proclaimed back. Fernanda had raved heavily about the actress on the way back from the RCS-JSP headquarters.

Daisy and Carmen went down the stairs and joined Fernanda and Ariella on the couch, starting the long process of getting ready for the party. As the movie went on, makeup products and girls alike began taking over the better part of the living room. It wasn't until about an hour later that they heard footsteps coming into the room. "Text Mom. I'm headed to Landon's house," Carlos called out.

"Whatever!" Fernanda called back.

Carmen's eyes widened in fear, and for a split second, Fernanda was confused. "His car! He's taking his car!" she whispered to the other girls. Everyone scrambled up.

Carlos turned around and looked confused, wondering why they cared about where he was going. "Is everything okay?"

Carmen shook her head, and everyone stopped talking, waiting for her excuse. "Fernanda was talking about how your mom...took the carrr..." She glanced at Fernanda, who understood and began to sneak over to where his keys were so that he wouldn't have a chance to grab them. "To get an oil change! Yeah, the thing had been beeping when she was about to go get milk," Carmen finished, hoping he didn't go check the garage. Carlos raised an eyebrow, questioning her odd story. Behind Carlos, Fernanda quietly held the keys and began creeping toward the garage.

"I told Mom to get eggs. We have enough milk," Carlos said, making Carmen snap her attention back to him. Carlos sighed, walking up the stairs. "I'll have to text her about it."

Fernanda opened the door that led to the garage, hearing the girls conversing behind her. All of the guests' eyes widened when they saw the bright red statement of a sports car. Its sunroof was off, and the tiny useless windows were tinted on each side. The black leather seats shone, and the white stitches really pulled the whole thing together. Fernanda clipped herself into the driver's seat before anyone could protest.

"Good Raji, that's gotta be over a hundred thousand! And for a first car?" Carmen said, whistling through her teeth.

Ariella and Daisy got in the back seat, and Carmen stood on the driver's side. "Move over, Fernanda. I'm driving."

Fernanda made a sour face. "Says who? It's my brother's car. I wanna drive! You can have shotgun."

Carmen gave her a look of disbelief. "Are you fucking with me? You barely passed your permit test and don't even have your license!" Maybe she'd been bragging too much about her permit to the other girls on the bus ride home from the JSP headquarters. Fernanda learned that they all had licenses except for Ariella, who didn't even have a permit.

"No way are you driving!" Carmen opened the door and tried to shove her over the console to the passenger's side, but Fernanda had been prepared, having strapped herself in to avoid being moved.

"I've been practicing. I know how to drive!" Fernanda protested, aimlessly flailing her foot around, trying to kick Carmen.

"Which includes almost running me over in my driveway!" Ariella called from the back, referencing how Fernanda had snuck out of the house to pick her up (with Carlos in the passenger's seat, mind you).

"I forgot how to stop the car then," Fernanda argued, starting the car up. "That was like three hours ago. I'm much better now."

Carmen gave her an incredulous look, trying to force her way into the driver's seat again. But as she did, her foot pressed against Fernanda's foot, which made her step on the gas pedal, and the car sprang forward…into the wall. The sickening sound of metal smashing into the wall made them all cringe. Everyone went silent.

"You don't think Carlos heard, right?" Ariella asked from the back seat in a small voice.

"What did you girls do?" they heard from inside the house.

Fernanda began trying to figure out how to back up, ready to make a quick getaway to the party. "Which pedal backs me up?"

"There's a pedal for that?" Daisy asked, beginning to panic from their current situation. "My mom says that you just use the knob for that!"

"No, you idiot! You need to use the gear stick!" Carmen said, practically yelling at them. She climbed over Fernanda's lap and into the passenger seat as the other girl began trying to find "the stick" in the incredibly modern car.

"Girls? Where are you?"

"Where is the damn stick!" Fernanda asked in a hushed voice.

Carmen sighed and twisted the knob to R. "Just step on the gas."

Carlos opened the door to the garage. "Girls? Are you…" His voice trailed off as he saw them all in his car, driver's side door wide open.

"Now!" Carmen yelled, making Fernanda jump and press her foot on the pedal.

They sped backward, the car beeping rapidly as the door flapped with their movements. Carlos took a couple of steps in the direction of the car before seeing Carmen changing the gears for Fernanda and speeding off. His sister took both hands off the wheel to slam the door, making her friends in the back scream at her. He shook his head, knowing that Fernanda was a terrible driver, and his car probably wouldn't make it through the night. "Queen Raji, help them." That's when his eyes saw the huge hole in the wall that the car made from speeding into the wall. "Scratch that. All of the RCS help them."

D AISY HAD NEVER BRUSHED UP to death before this. Not in real life at least. She wasn't sure she really wanted to do it again either. That's what the more reasonable brain cells were saying. She felt like screaming and vomiting at the same time, choking herself into a frenzy. But honestly, there was something freeing about speeding one hundred and ten miles an hour down an empty highway while blasting some revenge-based breakup song. The sunroof was put away, and everyone's hair was blowing wildly as Fernanda floored the pedal. It was dramatically fantastic to scream along to the lyrics, no matter how many times the artist repeated the same line over and over. It was almost like a movie where the main character drives off into the sunset, raising their middle fingers in the air as a giant *fuck you* to the world.

It was magnificent.

Then again, zooming down the highway at breakneck speed hadn't been the part where they almost died, even though one might assume that. They hadn't even almost died when Fernanda forgot that she was driving and raised her arms in the air to her "break-up anthem." Daisy was still trying to wrap her head around the fact that it was even remotely possible for her to forget that she was driving. She was also getting whiplash from how quickly Fernanda's opinions changed on how she felt about Jack. It was a little disorientating how someone's life could revolve so much around men. Just like Brittany.

But tonight was not about Brittany and how she may or may not have actually stayed home with JJ like she promised. Or about how JJ had anxiety about new people coming into the house and how having a new babysitter was not a good idea. Tonight was about her living life to the fullest. And apparently about testing the limits of how much adrenaline the human body could withstand.

Fernanda just had to forget that when you got off an empty highway, there were things called *other cars*. And those things did not go speeding by a red light at ninety-five miles per hour or try to take a U-turn in the middle of an intersection at eighty miles an hour. They also did not laugh at their passengers while doing this, saying things like "it's part of the party experience" and "the officials don't come over to these roads at this time anyway." Daisy was not sure if she should be concerned about the latter of those two.

The worst part wasn't even those things, sad as that may be. Lizzie lived in a gorgeous cliffside mansion. Her family also owned the fifty-plus acres that surrounded it and probably the "petite houses" as well (what the rich people liked to call the houses that normal people owned).

Fernanda claimed she knew a secret back road to get there faster because she'd gone to so many parties there. They should have trusted Lizzie's *best friend*, Carmen, when she told them that, no, that shortcut was not safe for people who liked to careen down the highway fifty miles over the speed limit. But they all could hear and see the fireworks coming from the top of the cliff, and they were scared to miss the best parts of the party. So yeah, they let Fernanda run them up a cliff in a car that probably was more suited to cruising around custom-made roads than climbing up a path that was rougher than a road full of speed bumps.

It was going fine when they were heading in a straight line uphill with Fernanda being a little too lenient on the gas pedal. And maybe, yeah, they all were so caught up in singing along to the man who insisted that his ex-girlfriend was a cougar instead of paying attention to the curve that someone plopped down in the road. Maybe she and Ariella screamed like their lives were flashing before their eyes when they saw the curve and the convenient lack of railings, not that it would've helped much at the speed they were going at.

Fernanda jerked the car towards the cliff wall, remembering to brake the car thanks to Carmen yelling at her from the passenger's seat. That right there proved to Daisy two things. One: Miracles were possible. Two: Fernanda López should never ever be allowed behind the wheel of a motorized vehicle again.

Once the car had come to a halt, Carmen let herself loose by laughing and closing her eyes, cackling for at least a minute straight. It was a little unsettling seeing someone laugh about the near-death experience they had all just shared, but it made sense in a twisted little way. Who knows, it may be one of those life-long bonding moments that stuck with her forever.

Fernanda peered down the side of the car at the scratch they'd placed from ramming it against the cliff. "The car looks like a hot mess." She groaned at the very visible mark. "I wanted to pull up with a nice car without a scratch."

Daisy almost asked her why this was her biggest worry out of all things this scratch could mean, starting with the fact that this was not their car and ending with Fernanda's parents tracking their location to pick up the car. Wait, did Fernanda's parents have her location? Oh, good Raji. They were in trouble if that were the case. She was almost afraid to ask, but she did anyway. "Do you share your location with your parents?"

It got very quiet before Fernanda yelled her millionth curse of the night. Carmen had her head in her hands, saying something about how this plan could not fall into any more pieces. Ariella flicked the back of her head, yelling about how she had cursed it. All the queen's horses and all the queen's men couldn't piece this night together again.

"Let's just assume they know," Daisy said out loud, not recognizing the strength that her voice held. "Do we wanna head back or at least have some fun first?" She hopped back in the car and gave Fernanda a small smile, cocking her head in the direction of the party.

Fernanda eventually started up the car again before her passengers could kick her out of the driver's seat. They drove at a respectable speed, and it took Daisy a good five minutes to convince her body that they were not about to die. They eventually pulled up to the house in all its white marble glory.

"It has a fucking fountain," Fernanda muttered under her breath, as though this were the worst atrocity committed by mankind. "A fucking stone lion with water pouring out of its mouth."

"Hurry up! I'm ready to party," Carmen insisted, voice borderline aggravated.

Fernanda let loose a grin and got out of her seat, leaving Carmen to curse at her for forgetting to place the car in park. Ariella scrambled out of her seat, jogging a little to catch up with the two girls. She linked arms with Daisy, and Fernanda raised a brow. "Do I just have to sit on the outside of two best friends?"

"I mean, you did almost kill us," Ariella told her unapologetically. "So..."

Daisy elbowed her and placed an arm through Fernanda's, all three girls walking to the party together. It started to get annoying when they realized just how long Lizzie's driveway was. It had a gorgeous cobblestone walkway and perfectly manicured bushes and flowers surrounding them, guiding them to the real gem on the property.

"Remind me that I need to vomit on these bushes before we leave," Fernanda announced, grabbing a handful of leaves with her silver and blue nails. They fluttered in the air like ashes, settling on the ground behind them. "Lizzie can't be allowed to have everything, can she?"

Daisy decided that Fernanda did not want her answer to that question and kept her mouth shut. Ariella did not. "Well," the girl said, gesturing at the grandness of the whole place, "looks like she already does."

Fernanda shot Ariella a nasty glare before snorting, "That'll end tonight."

Daisy gave her a questioning glance, suddenly on edge by the seriousness in her tone. "And how exactly will that end? We aren't doing anything to her, right?"

Fernanda scoffed, as this idea was completely ridiculous. "Jack broke up with her, so I'm gonna be here and get back together with him."

"I seriously don't see how you could go back to him," Ariella said, with the air of someone who'd been through many tumultuous relationships. Daisy knew that she'd never actually officially dated someone. "He obviously doesn't like you."

Fernanda hissed out a string of curses before narrowing her eyes on Ariella. "Have you ever even had a boyfriend?" She tilted her head and looked her up and down. "You don't really strike me as lesbian. Correct me if I'm wrong."

"I'm straight," Ariella confirmed, and Daisy knew from the grimace lines in the corner of her mouth that Fernanda was able to read her too well. It wasn't really a challenge to read her. She wore her emotions on her face. "I don't really think it's your business whether or not I've ever had a boyfriend before." She looked Fernanda up and down and then smirked. "Have you ever had a boyfriend besides Jack?"

Daisy sighed as Fernanda's face turned bright pink, knowing that yet another spat was about to ensue. "I don't think that my love life is any of your business," Fernanda shot at her. Daisy made sure to use her arms to lengthen the distance between the girls. "So stop pushing it."

Ariella snorted, and Daisy sighed, knowing exactly what her friend was thinking. "Youch!"

Fernanda's cheeks went from a light strawberry to full-on tomato. "Good fucking Queen of the RCS, could you be any more of a middle schooler?"

That comment triggered Ariella right where it was supposed to, and Daisy forcibly pushed her back from Fernanda. "Excuse me? You get to question my love life and sexuality and belittle me, but I can't do the same?" She was growling now. Daisy did not like the fact that she was always placed in the middle as the unofficial peacemaker. "I swear on my—"

"You're wearing my clothes," Fernanda interrupted. "And I can ask for them back at any time. Just something to think about if I were you." She was just full on discarding the limits, trying to see just how much she could get away with.

"You'd seriously violate my body by making me give up your clothes at a party?" Ariella asked, a harshness in her voice that Daisy had never really heard before. "You are such a bitch."

That, however, didn't seem to bother Fernanda, who only laughed before announcing, "Nothing I haven't heard before." She flicked her eyes over to Daisy as if sharing a joke between the two of them. "You could stand to get out of your comfort zone."

Daisy spoke before Ariella could respond, anticipating that this was about to get ugly. "Can both of you please stop?" She tried to give a chuckle, but it came out like a hacking sound. "Our real goal is to have fun."

Fernanda huffed. "I'm sorry that the girl over there is suffocating my cheerful vibes. It's really hard to cut through that gloom."

"Well, I'm sorry," Ariella began while examining her chipped orange polish, "that the girl with enough hair gel to last ten days is mood-swinging so hard that we're all getting whiplash."

Daisy almost snorted because Fernanda was indeed wearing a lot of hair gel. Her usual high ponytail was in a plaited braid to match the cowgirl theme she more-or-less had going on. But Fernanda would probably *insist* that she was taking sides, and they'd just start up all over again.

Something clapped her shoulders, hard enough to make her let go of both Fernanda's and Ariella's arms and take up an attack position of sorts, only to realize that it was Carmen. Carmen wobbled on her heels, grabbing onto Fernanda's outstretched arm and Daisy's hand. "My bad! I forgot you went to park the car," Daisy said apologetically.

Carmen flashed her a megawatt grin, finding her footing and linking her arms through Daisy's and Ariella's, being a divider between the two friends. Fernanda returned to her position at Daisy's other side, and Daisy was secretly grateful for the extra body between the two girls.

They walked in silence for a while with Daisy thinking about the way Lizzie's house got bigger and bigger the closer they got. Most houses got taller the closer you got, looking like anthills and growing into two-story living units, but this house seemed to get wider as well. Nothing was really obscuring their view when they were walking up to it. The house was like the sparkling diamond of a ring. Even Fernanda's house, which was the nicest house out of anyone Daisy personally knew, didn't get wider as she approached it. It was like a magic trick, making a rabbit appear out of thin air.

When they reached the house, Fernanda grabbed a sticky note off the door, reading it aloud: "'All are welcome.'" She squinted as though it were difficult to read the immaculate handwriting. "'The front door is unlocked. Just come right in.'" Fernanda crumbled the note up in her hand. "Oops, looks like the wind blew it away." She tossed it into the bush, and it looked like a neon pink flower in a sea of green.

Ariella tsked and opened the door, holding it open for the rest of the girls. "Are we gonna stand out here all night or go in?"

Fernanda grabbed the door handle from her, taking her spot and saying, "That's my line!"

Ariella scoffed and began taking off her shoes till Carmen told her that nobody cared about that because they'd be going in and out most of the night due to the fireworks. Unless someone started doing fireworks inside, which was also extremely likely.

Daisy looked around the room, taking in the fifteen-foot ceilings and the chandelier hanging from it like a rope. The area by the front door had so many coats and cover-ups by the door that Daisy was pretty sure things would get mixed up or stolen when people began to pour out, especially since most of them wouldn't be at peak sobriety. The quartet of girls made their way to the living room, which had perfectly white couches and coffee tables that glittered like diamonds.

"Remind me to spill some wine on the couches," Fernanda told them, running a hand over the soft cushions. "There's no way she can get the stains out of this fabric."

"Why would we have to remind you? I'd think that you'd have no trouble remembering that yourself," Carmen said. Daisy gave Carmen a look that was pleading to keep the fragile little peace they had, which she promptly ignored.

"Because I might be too drunk to remember all the things I need to spill shit on," Fernanda told her, rubbing her boot on the white rug stemming from underneath one of the couches. "There's too much perfection in this house. It's annoying."

Carmen only shrugged in return, leading the way to the makeshift bar in the kitchen. Daisy shouldn't have been shocked by the fact that the "makeshift" bar looked real enough to be in business, but she was. She took a seat on a stool by the counter.

A guy who barely looked old enough to be in high school came up to her. His blonde waves gave him an unflattering haircut. It looked a little bit like a brand new mop. "What package do you want?" he asked.

Carmen tapped Daisy on the shoulder, pointing at Ariella, who had a pained expression. Ariella mouthed the word "pads," and Daisy nodded. The pair traversed out of the room. She returned her attention to the person in front of her, confused. "What do you mean by package?"

He pointed at the blackboard above his head that was hanging from the ceiling. "Either pay twenty per person for unlimited drinks or three per drink."

Fernanda was at the counter in an instant, slamming her fist on the wooden ledge. It barely made a sound, and she grimaced at the splinter that was now stuck in her hand. "You're Lizzie's brother! You were in my Intro to Psych class." She paused before looking up at the sign that hung above the bar. "Is your sister seriously charging for the shitty drinks at her own party?" She grabbed a glass from behind the bar and almost slammed it to pieces before coming to her senses. "I bet she isn't even paying you!"

Daisy looked at the boy in front of her more carefully, trying to find a resemblance between him and the girl in their grade. Their noses looked similar, and they were both natural blondes. Let's be honest, it was easy to spot a fake blonde when you came across one. She looked into his eyes, recognizing the shape, but his eyes were brown, different from Lizzie's glacier blue orbs.

"Are you done staring at me?" he deadpanned.

Daisy realized that he was still a person and that her eyes had been drilling into his for quite a while. "Sorry," she told him. "I was just trying to find a resemblance to Lizzie in your face. I would've never guessed that she had a brother."

He made a loose tsking sound before pointing up at the blackboard. "What'll it be?"

Daisy sighed and pulled out her phone. "Twenty, I guess. Might be coming back here a lot." She paid with her phone and asked, "Are you her little brother? You look like you're in middle school."

Fernanda snorted loudly, unapologetically blowing a gloop of snot onto the wood. He sighed and placed two glasses of clear liquid in front of the two girls. "It's water. I promise," he said reassuringly.

Daisy sniffed it before deciding to take a sip. He was right, and she took a bigger gulp. "Can I have vodka lemonade? Lots of sweetness please," Fernanda demanded, her water already gone.

He held out the payment transfer device. "Three or twenty?"

Fernanda gave him a nasty look before realizing he wasn't going to budge when it came to the payment. "Twenty, but tell your sister she's a 'effed up person for charging for drinks at a party when you're both filthy rich."

He only snorted. A *knowing* snort, which let Daisy know he wouldn't be talking with Lizzie about this anytime soon. "How much did she give you?" Daisy asked while he began his special process of mixing and stirring to create Fernanda's drink. "I mean for making the drinks."

He placed a sprig of mint in the cup before finishing it off with a large ice cube. "I get seventy percent, and she gets thirty. It was her idea anyway." He looked as though he were about to slide the drink before remembering that it was on a bumpy wooden counter.

"I can't believe she gets money for just stumbling around like a lost chihuahua," Fernanda said, taking a swig of her drink and almost gagging. "You're the one making it all. Don't you ever wanna party yourself?"

"Have you ever tried talking to Lizzie?" he asked incredulously, ignoring the last question. "I know you both hate each other's guts and all, but you've got to know how ridiculously stubborn she can be."

Daisy pointed a finger at Fernanda, saying, "If anyone can match Lizzie's stubbornness, it's that girl."

He eyed her face up and down before seeming to come to an internal agreement. "Why are you even here?" He held up a finger as she opened her mouth. "Don't give some BS excuse about wanting to barf all on the carpet. You do that at every party." He leaned in towards Daisy and fake whispered, "She can't hold her liquor."

Fernanda took another swig of her drink as though the effects of it weren't coming in fast enough. "Not true by the way. I just choose to vomit." She drained the last bits through teeth so white they could cut through the darkest night. "It's even better because I don't remember crap about it, so it's not my problem."

Daisy looked her up and down, a wave of concern passing over her. "You mean you often get blackout drunk?"

Fernanda shrugged and placed her glass on the wood. "And if I do?"

Lizzie's brother picked it up and gave it back to her filled with water. She narrowed her eyes at him, and he jutted his head at Daisy. "She's right. A cup of water between each drink." He sighed and began filling up Daisy's glass with a clear bubbly liquid. "It'll help slow it down. You can only have a certain amount of liquid in your body at once anyway." He looked at Daisy and pointed his chin at her drink. Most guys thought they looked cool doing something like that, but he did it so smoothly that she almost didn't notice it. "Lemon-lime soda. You don't seem like a cherry soda type."

Daisy admired the neon green and yellow rock candy on her glass. "Did you just add this on?" she questioned, unsure of how she didn't notice him placing the candy on her glass. "If so, that was pretty quick."

He let out a snort because boys like him wouldn't be caught dead cackling like a witch. His face had barely changed expressions since they'd been there. "I pre-made these cups. It takes a while for the honey to dry enough where the rocks won't move."

Daisy nodded. That explanation made more sense to her. "I do like cherry soda." She wasn't sure why she felt the need to explain this, but the words kept coming out. "But lemon-lime is fine too. Just thought I'd say that."

He seemed to take that with a slight surprise but said nothing after that, turning his attention back to Fernanda. "Why are you here?"

She made a vague gesture someone does when they are about to run a loop around your question while hoping you fall for it. "It's a girls' night, and y'all were supposed to have free drinks. So," she winked, "I brought my new gang here."

"You didn't have a gang before," he deadpanned. Daisy began choking violently. "And I call BS on your reason."

This guy was better at figuring out Fernanda than Daisy gave him credit for, so she decided to give him a hint. "We're here for backup."

He grabbed Fernanda's empty glass of water (Daisy was honestly impressed with how quickly her cup was drained) and gave her a knowing smile. "Ah, Lizzie was ranting on the phone about the chocolates." He shook his head. "Dickhead's outside by the fireworks."

"He's not a dick," Fernanda tried to say, but she was already getting up and out of her seat. "But I think I'll be going now." She held out her hand for the next drink: a brown bubbly liquid. "Follow me if you want, Daisy. I'll be nonchalantly lighting a firework."

Daisy wasn't sure if she was more unsettled that Fernanda didn't specify if the firework would be outside or the fact that she was attempting to do it "nonchalantly." Or both. Both deserved concern. She got up and sighed, taking her soda with her. Lizzie's brother grabbed her wrist for a second, and she turned to him, confused.

"Keep an eye on Fernanda for *all* our sakes," he said, his other hand fingering the top button on his shirt.

She pulled her wrist away from his grasp but stayed there, waiting for a better explanation. But he only started wiping down the wooden counter, eyes meticulously scanning it for stains that weren't there. "Why?"

He scoffed and turned away from her, washing out a dirty cup Daisy hadn't seen before. "Jack's a pretty shitty guy, and when he leaves her again…and he will. Mark my words… it'll be ugly."

Daisy nodded, then spoke up when she remembered his back was towards her. "Thanks for the advice, I guess."

He nodded. Daisy disappeared down the hallway, heading for the door. It was going to be a very long night.

Four and a Half Years Earlier...

Same thing each day.

Scary. Scary. Scary.

"Come here."

Needles, scary. Wires, scary.

"No, I don't wanna. Too scary."

Shaking. Tears. Sad.

"It'll be okay. Just come here and let me just poke you a tiny bit. It won't even hurt."

Needles, scary.

"I want my mom! I want Dad!"

Wet. Salty. Tears. I lick them away.

"Sweetheart, Mommy isn't coming back for you. Neither is Dad. They forgot about you. They don't care about you anymore. Now, come over here and get your shot."

Cry. Shiver. Weak.

"No."

Strong?

"You don't say no to me."

There is no room for questioning. Do as he says, or I'll regret it.

Needle. Stab. Scream. Smack.

"Rule number one: When you don't listen, that's what happens. You understand?"

Wet. Salty.

Red?

Not the red that the scary needles and wires are taking out of me. Not the red mark his palm leaves on my cheek. It is a little shape dancing in the dark. The Voice is what I call it.

Scritchy scritchy scratch, says the Voice inside, asking to see the outside.

"That hurts," I say back. Not to him. To It.

"Almost done, sweetie. You're being such a good girl." The words sound like eating too much ice cream on a hot day. They make the Voice poke and scratch more.

Needles, out. Wires, gone.

"Now, we need to run some tests, but from what I've been seeing, I think you're the key, sweetheart!"

He was the one who took me. He gets to call me sweetheart now?

Scritchy scritchy **poke**, the Voice goes, demanding to leave.

"Ow! Stop!" I say back.

Grandfather gives me a look of annoyance, ignoring his test tubes of my red and other substances. "It's over, okay? You can shut up now."

"I wasn't talking to you. You don't care about—"

Smack. Sting. ~~Sadness.~~ Spark.

"Rule number two: No back talk. I find it annoying."

I am nothing to him. Just something to test and experiment on. Like your volcano for a science project or the rock you break open to see the shiny colors. I never mattered anyway. That's what Grandfather says.

The Voice begins to get restless, running around and *scritchy scritchy* **poking** everywhere. My breathing follows, trying to copy the endless energy the Voice has.

In. Out. Faster.

Breathing goes faster as the Voice begins *scritchy scratch* **scraping**.

In. In. Out. Out. Faster.

My heart begins to join the Voice. *Bounce bounce jumping* everywhere.

In. In. In. Out. Out. Out.

"Stop!" I scream in a panic, my breathing uncontrollable. "Stay still!"

But It won't listen, trying to tear a hole for itself and my heart to go outside.

Thump. Ground. Rolling. Screaming. *Scritchy* **poke rip**!

It almost wins, transforming my hands into things sharp and soft, like a kitten.

Scream. Smack. Sting. ~~Spark.~~ Yellow.

Two red marks, one for each cheek. Perfectly matching the other.

In. In. In. Out. Oouuttt. Calmer, slower.

In. In. Oouuttt. Slow, normal.

In. Out.

I put a hand to my face. It feels warm. And hurts. A lot.

I hear the Voice in the back of my head, begging, pleading.

What was It?

What did It want?

Was the Voice the reason I'm here?

I am, It says, surprising me with speaking actual words. I almost scream but control myself, not wanting more red marks on my cheeks.

It chuckles. *I can speak when I want to. Do you think I only talk about my actions all the time? That'd be boring.*

"Why?" I madly whisper, making sure Grandfather isn't looking. He's too busy with my red. "Why did you make them take me?"

*First off, your logic is completely off. They took you because I'm **inside** you. But I can't leave you. I'm always here and always have been.*

"How?" I ask, and also add quickly, "Why did you start speaking now?"

Too many questions. Just let me out. I close my eyes and try to get close to the red shape dancing in the dark, teasing me with Its freedom from being stuck on the inside.

Nothing happens.

"How do I let you out?" I ask quietly, eyes back open.

The only reply is: *You'll know how when you want to. Poof! I'll come again when you need me.*

I feel It leave, Its shape laughing as it runs.

"Stupid," I mutter. "You'll know how when you want to."

~~Grandfather~~ He turns toward me. "Who are you talking to, sweetheart?"

Sting. ~~Yellow.~~ Orange.

"Nobody."

Pitiful. Weak. Nothing.

"Good. Remember, I don't like backtalk." He goes back to his endless cycle of pouring and mixing. "When I'm talking to my co-workers, you're…Asset 1115."

"But I have a name. The one you gave me. Isn't that enough?" But it isn't. It never is.

Sigh. Annoyance.

I feel stupid for asking, like I should have already known by now.

"But we're trying to find out who you are. Heck, what you are. You're the key we've been looking for."

It all makes sense. The Voice is right. It all links back to It. I half expect It to pop up and tease me for not realizing sooner, but It decides to stay quiet for once.

"I don't get what you're trying to say," I say, pretending.

He seems happy, talking a lot more than usual. But of course, I am nothing, so it didn't matter what he says to me about his plans. "You're not normal, sweetheart. I should've known it all along. You have the key in you! Now, with your help," he pokes me in the gut playfully, "the RCS finally has the edge it's been looking for!"

He wants to trap me forever.

EPILOGUE

~~Once there was a family of two parents and two children, and they were happy.~~

Once there was a family of two grandparents and two children, and they weren't happy. They had two parents, who were both off on a grand honeymoon.

It was fine during the day, playing with puzzles, building with wooden bricks, and lots of other old people things that they believed kids liked. But when they were put to bed without speaking to their parents for the third time in a row, the younger one felt on edge.

The darkness was different this time. It wasn't the calm, peaceful mist that would take them to dreamland. It was a tumultuous wave, drowning them in terrors and shaking them violently. The younger one didn't realize they were screaming like a devil possessed them until they saw the older one's face looking down at them.

Nothing wrong happened, they told the older one. Just a terrible, terrible nightmare. Nothing that was real. It all happened in that dreamworld where all the monsters tried to grab you but couldn't. Except that the younger one wasn't so sure that all the monsters were going to stay there. They might cross over from their dreams to reality.

The grandma appeared in the doorway, taking in the state of her youngest grandchild, and gasped. Milk and cookies were the only thing to fix such a situation, she proclaimed, grabbing the younger one out of the bed and taking them to the kitchen. Milk and cookies were the best way to fix those dreams.

And so they went, mixing in flour and sugar and just a tiny pinch of salt into the mix. The younger one poured in the chocolate chips and the teaspoon of vanilla. It was hypnotic to watch the wet ingredients mix with the dry ones. It was soothing to scoop the cookies into perfect half-cup balls, pressing them down into heart-shaped goodness. Why a heart, the younger one asked when the grandma first used her fingers to make the shape. Why not a regular circle?

Because they loved each other, the grandma explained, helping the younger one move their hands to make the correct shape. Because they would always be together in their hearts. It was a nice thought, a thought that made all the monsters and creepers crawl away. It was always safe here in the house.

They both watched the cookies rise up for ten minutes before falling as they cooled off on the rack. The grandma got out the plates and cups while the younger one reached for the milk in the fridge. Three cookies for the younger one, four for Grandma. A perfect seven. The milk was poured to the rim in the glasses, perfect for the curly straws that the grandma had. But the grandma grabbed a bottle, slipping her slender fingers down the neck and coming out with the perfect amount of white powder. It's a special sugar, she told the younger one with a smile. Little kids love it, but it's too sweet for grandmas and grandpas. She cocked her head at the younger one, asking if they wanted the special sugar.

The younger one clapped their hands delightedly and nodded, excited for the sugary overload that was sure to happen. The powder slid in, and with a flick of a curly straw, no one would have ever known that a little bit of sweetness was added.

A bite of cookie. A sip of milk. Dunk the cookie in the milk. Bite it. An extra-large bite of cookie. Two sips of milk. The younger one's eyelids drooped, sleep catching up and trying to overtake them. The grandma handed her grandchild the leftover milk and cookie. Just a few more bites. They don't want to waste the special treat, do they? Three bites of cookie. Two sips of milk. One last one, the grandma insisted pleasantly. You can go to sleep afterward.

So the younger one did, and they let their head drop drowsily against the table. In the living room, which felt so far away at the moment, the grandfather clock rang three times. The younger one's eyes closed for good when the final toll rang out, and the grandma grabbed the cookies and milk, dumping them both down the drain, never to see the light of day again.

She cocooned the younger one in her arms, brushing the hair off their upper lip and rubbing excess powder on to give them the sweetest sleep of their life. She looked at the child's face with an upward twitch of her lips. Somewhere in the house, a floorboard creaked, and it broke the spell.

They both disappeared into the dark that night, the younger to never see that house again. The grandma came back. The powder was disposed of, and a grief-stricken face was placed on. The monsters had finally gotten to the younger one like they were warned, and they would not let go of *her* for a long time.

ACKNOWLEDGEMENTS

While writing this book, I did *not* take into account that writing is not a quick process. You can't just sit down and say, *I wanna write a book this week* and have it be a finished piece of work that you're proud of. At least, I know I can't. You can, however, speed up the process. I'd like to thank the people who helped expedite the process. My mom always encouraged me whenever I had writer's block, helping me distinguish it from times when I was just trying to get out of typing away on the computer. My dad and younger sister were also there, willing to bounce around ideas or answer out of pocket questions whenever I needed a quick second opinion. I'd also like to thank Katy Lei, my editor, designer, and marketer, who helped me find that fine line between fantasy and reality. She let me know when I had gone off the rails and when I needed to dive more deeply into that imaginative world. Other people who have been amazing support are my high school Lit & Comp teachers who are always there to listen to my ramblings and will be blessed with the very first copies of my experiment.

ABOUT THE AUTHOR

Zoey Sweet lives in the Pacific Northwest and loves writing, reading, and running. She does not have any pets but really wants a husky and two cats when she gets older. Her favorite book series is *The Naturals*, and her favorite author is Jennifer Lynn Barnes. Her passion for writing stemmed from when she learned how to write her name at two. As she got older, she realized that if she wanted to be good at something, she had to start young, thus driving her start as an author.

To keep up to date with the author, go to zoeyasweet.com and @zoeysweetwrites on Instagram.

www.ingramcontent.com/pod-product-compliance
Lightning Source LLC
LaVergne TN
LVHW011937070526
838202LV00054B/4697